CW00863441

This book belongs to

....

Five-minute Toy Stories

Compiled by
Tig Thomas

MILES
KELLY

First published in 2018 by Miles Kelly Publishing Ltd
Harding's Barn, Bardfield End Green, Thaxted, Essex, CM6 3PX, UK

This edition printed 2019

2 4 6 8 10 9 7 5 3

Publishing Director Belinda Gallagher
Creative Director Jo Cowan
Editorial Director Rosie Neave
Senior Editor Sarah Parkin
Senior Designer Joe Jones
Image Manager Liberty Newton
Production Elizabeth Collins, Jennifer Brunwin-Jones
Reprographics Stephan Davis, Callum Ratcliffe-Bingham
Assets Lorraine King

ISBN 978-1-78617-868-8

Printed in China

British Library Cataloguing-in-Publication Data
A catalogue record for this book is available from the British Library

ACKNOWLEDGEMENTS

The publishers would like to thank the following artists who have contributed to this book:
Advocate Art: Milena Jahier, Claire Keay, Bruno Merz, Kimberley Scott
Sophia Touliatou (cover)
Beehive Illustration: Rupert Van Wyk (inc. decorative frames)
All other artwork from the Miles Kelly Artwork Bank

Made with paper from a sustainable forest

www.mileskelly.net

Contents

Adventures and Troubles

Child's Play

About the Artists

Milena Jahier works using mixed media and often finishes her illustrations off digitally. When she is looking for ideas, either a quick catnap or a walk will often do the trick. Of all the different languages Milena speaks, illustration is her all time favourite.

The Grandmother of the Dolls, Finding Raggedy Andy, Jedidiah's Noah's Ark, Sara finds Emily, Take's Birthday, Teddy has an Adventure, Hitty and the Crow, The Racketty-Packetty House in Trouble

Claire Keay works from her small studio at home in Essex. She illustrates with pen and watercolour, although recently she has started to enjoy painting digitally, too. Claire says she loves illustrating children's books because it allows your imagination to run a little wild, and you don't have to follow too many rules!

The Toys in the Wood, My Making, Bessie's Doll, Adventure in the Attic, Raggedy Andy to the Rescue, Tom Sawyer at Play, Patty Pans

Bruno Merz was born in New Zealand, where he studied traditional animation. After working in France and The Netherlands, he now lives in England. Bruno spends his days illustrating children's books and writing music.

Pinocchio Comes to Life, The Dolls' Hospital, The Tin Soldier, A Family Christmas, The Top and the Ball, Trouble with Tar Marbles, A Jolly Good Game, A Surprise Party

Kimberley Scott begins her illustrations by hand, using a mixture of pencil, pen and ink. She then uses her computer to bring her characters to life with colour. Pattern, detail and a slight skew-whiff essence are key to Kimberley's work.

Philip Builds the Magic City, The Magic Sled, The Kite Tells his Tale, The Dolls and the other Dolls, Playing with Fire, Grandma's Christmas Gifts, Playing at Jungle Book, A Paper Doll's House

Rupert Van Wyk works between London and Italy. Using an ink dip pen and working on a light table, he tries to keep the lines as spontaneous as possible, and then uses watercolours to bring his images to life. The work of Quentin Blake is always a wonderful source of inspiration.

Decorative frames, The Visit to Santa Claus Land, The Racketty-Packetty House, Raggedy Ann and the Kittens, Sam's Earthquake, The Steadfast Tin Soldier, Trapped in Toytown, Kikeri

About the Authors

Find information below on some of the authors whose stories appear in this book.

LOUISA MAY ALCOTT 1832–1888
Little Women is Louisa May Alcott's most famous book. She began it in the hope it might pay off some of her family's debts. In it, she told stories about her childhood with her sisters.

HANS CHRISTIAN ANDERSEN 1805–1875
One of the greatest storytellers of all time, Hans Christian Andersen was a shy, difficult man who led a sad life, which is often reflected in his stories.

JOHN KENDRICK BANGS 1862–1922
A journalist and writer, John Kendrick Bangs became Editor for Humour at *Harper's Magazine*, *Harper's Bazaar* and *Harper's Young Folks*, a very popular magazine for young children.

FRANCES HODGSON BURNETT 1849–1924
Best-known for her classic children's book *The Secret Garden*, Frances Hodgson Burnett was brought up in Manchester, but moved to Tennessee in her teens.

CARLO COLLODI 1826–1890
Born in Florence, Italy, Carlo Collodi took his pen name from his mother's home town in Italy. His real surname was Lorenzini.

SUSAN COOLIDGE 1845–1905
During the American Civil War (1861–1865), Susan Coolidge worked as a nurse, before becoming a successful writer for children. Her greatest success was the popular story *What Katy Did*.

RACHEL FIELD 1894–1942
Hitty is Rachel Field's best-known book. It won the Newbery Medal in 1930 and was dedicated to the State of Maine.

JOHNNY GRUELLE 1880–1938
Artist and author Johnny Gruelle was inspired to create the Raggedy Ann books after his daughter, Marcella, found a dusty doll in the attic.

JOEL CHANDLER HARRIS 1848–1908
With eight children of his own, Joel Chandler Harris loved writing for them. He created the wonderful character of Brer Rabbit in his Uncle Remus stories.

MRS MOLESWORTH 1839–1921
Mary Louisa Molesworth wrote almost 100 books for children, and used to try out her stories on her own children.

LUCY MAUD MONTGOMERY 1874–1942
After her mother died when she was two, Lucy Maude Montgomery was sent to live with her grandparents on Prince Edward Island. Her most beloved character is Anne of Green Gables.

E NESBIT 1858–1924
Edith Nesbit wrote over forty fiction books for children, and created the idea of mixing real-life children in home settings with magical elements. One of her best-known books is *The Railway Children*.

MARK TWAIN 1835–1910
Starting work at twelve years old, Mark Twain became a printer, which led to him writing for newspapers. One of his most famous books is *The Adventures of Huckleberry Finn*.

CAROLYN WELLS 1862–1942
Including detective fiction, children's books, poetry and humour, Carolyn Wells wrote over 170 books.

EVELYN MAUDE WHITAKER 1844–1929
An English writer who published many books for young children, Evelyn Maude Whitaker also ran a holiday home for sick children.

Magical Moments

11

Pinocchio Comes to Life

An extract from *Pinocchio*
by Carlo Collodi

A poor old man called Geppetto has decided to carve a puppet.
He has brought home a lump of wood to make a start.

GEPPETTO LIVED IN a small ground-
floor room. The furniture could not
have been simpler – a bad chair, a poor bed
and a broken-down table. At the end of the
room there was a fireplace with a lit fire, but

the fire was painted. By the fire was a painted saucepan, which was boiling cheerfully and sending out a cloud of smoke that looked exactly like real smoke.

As soon as Geppetto reached his home, he took his tools and set to work to cut out and model his puppet.

"What name shall I give him?" Geppetto said to himself, "I think I will call him Pinocchio."

Having found a name for his puppet, Geppetto began to work. First he made his hair, then his forehead and then his eyes.

Once the eyes were finished, imagine how surprised Geppetto was when he saw that they moved and looked hard at him.

Geppetto, seeing himself stared at by

those two wooden eyes, said in an angry voice, "Wicked wooden eyes, why do you look at me?"

No one answered.

Then he started to carve the nose, but no sooner had he made it than it began to grow. It grew and grew and grew, until in a few minutes it had become an immense nose that seemed as if it would never end.

Geppetto tired himself out with cutting it off.

But the more he cut and shortened it, the longer the nose became!

The mouth was not even completed when it began to laugh and mock him.

"Stop laughing!" Geppetto ordered, but he might as well have spoken to the wall.

"Stop laughing, I say!" he roared in a threatening tone.

The mouth then stopped laughing, but put out its tongue as far as it would go.

Geppetto, not wanting to spoil his handiwork, pretended not to see and continued his work. After the mouth he carved the chin, then the throat, shoulders, stomach, arms and hands.

The hands were scarcely finished when Geppetto felt his wig snatched from his head. He turned round and saw his yellow wig in the puppet's hand.

"Pinocchio! Give me back my wig!"

But Pinocchio, instead of returning it, put it on his own head.

Geppetto cried out, "You young rascal! You are not yet completed, and you are already beginning to disobey your father! That is bad, my boy, very bad." And he dried a tear.

The legs and feet remained to be done.

When Geppetto had finished the feet, he received a kick on the point of his nose.

"I deserve it!" he said to himself, "I should have thought of it sooner. Now it is too late."

He then took the puppet under the arms

and placed him on the floor to teach him how to walk.

Pinocchio's legs were stiff and he could not move, but Geppetto led him by the hand and showed him how to put one foot in front of the other.

When his legs became flexible, Pinocchio began to walk all by himself and to run about the room. Then, having gone out of the door, the puppet jumped into the street and escaped.

Poor Geppetto rushed after him, but was not able to overtake him, for that rascal Pinocchio leapt in front of him like a hare! Knocking his wooden feet together against the pavement, Pinocchio made as much clatter as twenty pairs of metal toecaps.

"Stop him! Stop him!" shouted Geppetto. But the people in the street, seeing a wooden puppet running like a racehorse, stood still in astonishment to look at it, and laughed and laughed and laughed, until it beats description.

At last, by sheer luck, a policeman happened to come along, who, hearing all that noise, thought that it might be a runaway horse. He stood bravely in the middle of the street, with his legs wide apart, firmly determined to stop it.

Pinocchio saw the policeman and tried his best to escape between the legs of the big fellow, but without success.

The policeman grabbed him by the nose (it was an extremely long one and seemed

made on purpose for that very thing) and returned him to Geppetto.

The little old man wanted to twist Pinocchio's ears. Think how he felt when, upon searching for them, he discovered that he had forgotten to make them!

All he could do was seize Pinocchio by the back of the neck and take him home. As he was doing so, he shook him two or three times and said to him angrily, "We're going home now!"

The Grandmother of the Dolls

By Joel Chandler Harris

SUSAN HAD A GREAT many dolls and she was very fond of them. She had a china doll, a Japanese doll, a rag doll, a rubber doll, a white doll, a brown doll and a black doll. Every evening Susan carried the dolls into the bedroom and placed them side by side against the wall, so she could

21

see them last thing at night and first thing in the morning.

One night, when Susan was lying in bed, she heard a voice call out, "Oh, dear! I believe I've got soot all over my frock again!"

It was the queerest little voice that ever was heard. Just as she was wondering where it came from, a little old woman stepped down from the chimney and shook the ashes from her dress.

"I think I'd better stay at home," said the little old woman, "if I can't come down the chimney without getting dirt all over my frock. I wonder where Mr Thimblefinger is."

"Oh, I'm here," exclaimed another voice, "but I'm not coming down. I see the big black cat in that chair there."

"Much I care!" cried the little old woman snappishly. Then she touched the dolls with her cane, one by one. Each doll called out as it was touched, "Is that you, Granny?"

And to each one she replied, "Reser, roser, rise! And rib and rub your eyes!"

The dolls arose and arranged themselves in front of the fireplace, all except the rag doll.

"Where's Rag-Tag?" inquired the little

old woman, anxiously.

"Here I am, Granny!" replied the rag doll. "I'm lame in one leg and I can't walk with the other."

"Tut! Tut!" said the little old woman. "How can you be lame in your legs when there's no bone in them? Get up!"

Rag-Tag rolled out of the corner and tumbled across the floor, head over heels.

"Now, then," said the little old woman, "what can I do for you?"

"She's pulled all my hair out!" said the china doll.

"She's mashed my nose flat!" cried the Japanese doll.

"She's put one of my eyes out!" whined the brown doll.

"She's put chalk all over me!" blubbered the black doll.

"She hasn't hurt me!" exclaimed the rubber doll.

"She's made a hole in my back, and the sawdust is all running out!" whined Rag-Tag.

"I'll attend to you first," said the little old woman, frowning. Then she cried out, "Long-Legged Spinner, come and earn your dinner!"

While Susan was wondering what this meant, she saw a big black spider swing down from the ceiling and hang, dangling close to the little old woman's face.

"A thimbleful of fresh cobwebs, Long-Legged Spinner!" said the little old woman.

The spider moved its legs faster than a cat can wink its eyes, and in a few seconds the fresh cobwebs were spun.

"That is very nice," said the little old woman. "Here's a fat bluebottle for you."

With the fresh cobwebs, the little old woman quickly stopped the hole in Rag-Tag's back. This done, she went around and doctored each doll. She glued more hair on the china doll. She fixed the nose of the Japanese doll. She gave a new blue eye to the brown doll.

"There!" she exclaimed when she had finished, "I think you look a little more like

yourselves now. Now pay attention all of
you! What is the name of this horrible
giantess that drags you about and treats
you so badly?"

"It's no giantess, Granny," replied Rag-
Tag. "It's a little girl, and sometimes she's
very, very good."

"Hush!" cried the little old woman.

"She is a giantess, Granny," exclaimed
the brown doll. "She is even taller than that
chair there!"

"Where is she now?" the little old
woman asked fiercely.

"She's asleep in the bed, Granny," said
the brown doll.

"Pinch her good, Granny!" cried the
rubber doll.

"Scratch her, Granny! Pull out her hair!" pleaded the brown doll.

"Bump her head against the wall, Granny! Mash her nose!" exclaimed the Japanese doll.

Rag-Tag said not a word.

Susan began to feel frightened. Just then, her black cat that had been sleeping quietly in a chair, jumped to the floor and walked back and forth, rubbing against the little old woman.

"Stop," exclaimed the big black cat. "I know what you are here for. Do you see my teeth? They are as strong as iron. Do you see my claws? They are as sharp as needles. If I bite you, you'll squeal, if I scratch you, you'll bleed."

The Grandmother of the Dolls looked at the big black cat long and hard.

"What is your name?" she asked.

"Billy-Billy Blackfoot."

"It is time for you to go hunting," she said. The little old woman wanted to get him out of the room.

"I have found what I was hunting for," said Billy-Billy Blackfoot.

"There's a pan of milk in the kitchen."

"It won't turn sour before I drink it."

"There's catnip in the garden."

"It will grow till I want it."

The Grandmother of the Dolls then made a cross-mark on the carpet and waved her cane in the air. This was done to put a spell on the big black cat, but before

the spell could work, Billy-Billy Blackfoot
made a circle by chasing his tail around.
The Grandmother of the Dolls seized her
cane and made a furious attack on Billy-
Billy Blackfoot, but he leapt out of the way
and the cane fell with a whack on the bald
head of the brown doll.

At this there was a tremendous uproar.
The brown doll screamed, the dolls
scrambled and scurried under the bed, the
cat got ready to pounce, and the little old
woman whisked up the chimney like a

spark from a burning log.

When Susan sat up in bed to look around, Billy-Billy Blackfoot was sitting by the fireplace washing his face as quietly as if nothing had happened.

At first it seemed to Susan that it had all been a dream, but presently she heard a small voice that came down the chimney.

"Mr Thimblefinger! Mr Thimblefinger! It is nine minutes after twelve."

There was a pause, and then the small voice sounded farther away, "Nine minutes and two seconds after twelve!"

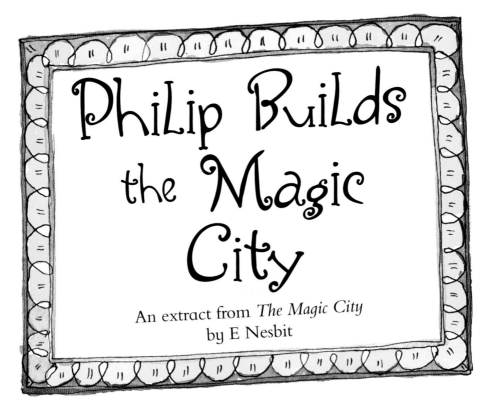

Philip Builds the Magic City

An extract from *The Magic City*
by E Nesbit

*Philip lives with his sister Helen, who has just married a man
with a daughter of his own, called Lucy. While Helen is on her
honeymoon, Philip has been left alone in the man's large house
with the servants. The room he likes best is the nursery.*

THE GREAT HOUSE was his to go to and
fro in. But he was not allowed to
touch anything in it. The nursery was the
room that attracted him the most, for it was
full of the most fascinating toys. A rocking

horse as big as a pony, the finest dolls' house you ever saw, boxes of tea things, boxes of bricks, puzzle maps, dominoes, chessmen, draughts – every kind of toy or game that you have ever had or ever wished to have. And Philip was not allowed to play with any of them.

"You mustn't touch anything," the nurse said. "The toys are Miss Lucy's. No – I can't give you permission to play with them."

For two whole days he lived at the Grange, hating it and everyone in it. And suddenly everything changed. The nurse got a message. A brother who had been thought to be drowned at sea had come home. She must go to see him.

In a happy bustle she packed and went.

At the last moment, Philip sprang forward.

"Oh, Nurse!" he cried, "Nurse, do say I may take Lucy's toys to play with. It is so lonely here."

Perhaps the nurse's heart was softened by her own happiness. At any rate, she answered, "Take anything you like. Goodbye everybody!"

Philip drew a deep breath, went straight up to the nursery, took out all the toys, and looked at every single one of them. It took him all the afternoon.

The next day he looked at all the things

34

again and longed to make something with them. He and Helen had built many a city out of his own two boxes of bricks and other things they had found in the house – dominoes, chessmen, cardboard boxes, books, lids of kettles and teapots. But they had never had enough bricks. Lucy had enough bricks for anything.

Philip began to build a city on the nursery table. But to build with bricks alone is poor work when you have been used to building with all sorts of other things.

"It looks like a factory," said Philip. "There must be something downstairs that would come in useful," he told himself, "and she did say, 'Take anything you like.'"

Philip carried down the boxes of bricks and the boxes of blocks, the draughts, the chessmen, and the box of dominoes. He took them into the long drawing room where the crystal chandeliers were, and the many long, light windows. He cleared a big writing table and began to build.

A bronze Egyptian god on a black-and-gold cabinet seemed to be looking at him from across the room.

"All right," said Philip. "I'll build you a temple. You wait a bit."

The bronze god waited and the temple grew. Two silver candlesticks, topped by chessmen, made pillars. Philip made a journey to the nursery to fetch the Noah's

Ark animals – the pair of elephants, each standing on a brick, flanked the entrance. It looked splendid, like an Assyrian temple in the pictures Helen had shown him. More Noah's Ark animals added an Egyptian-looking finish to the building.

"Ain't it pretty!" said Susan, the parlour maid, who came to call him to tea. "You are clever Master Philip, I will say that for you. But you'll get in big trouble for taking all them things."

"It doesn't hurt things by building with them," said Philip. "My sister and I always did it at home."

"Well," said Susan, "it's just like them postcards my brother in India sends me. I don't know how you think of such things."

Praise is sweet. Philip slipped his hand into that of the parlour maid as they went down the wide stairs to the hall, where tea awaited him.

"He's not half a bad child. You slip in and look at what he's been building," said Susan to the other servants. They did slip in, all of them, when Philip had gone to bed.

Next day, Philip went on with his building. He put everything you can think of into it – the dominoes and the domino box, bricks and books, cotton reels that he begged from Susan, and some cake tins sent by the cook. He made steps of the dominoes and a terrace of the domino box. Philip got bits of lavender out of the garden and stuck them in the cotton reels, which made beautiful pots, and they looked like bay trees in tubs. Brass bowls made domes, and the lids of brass kettles and coffee pots made minarets. Chessmen were useful for minarets, too.

"I must have paved paths and a fountain," said Philip. The paths were paved with mother-of-pearl counters.

The fountain was a silver-and-glass ashtray, with a little case of silver rising up from the middle of it. The falling water was made out of narrow bits of silver paper.

Palm trees were easily made (Helen had shown him how) with bits of larch fastened to elder stems with plasticine. There was plenty of plasticine among Lucy's toys – there was plenty of everything.

And the city grew, until it covered the table. Philip set about making another city on another table. This had a great water tower, with a fountain round its base. It was even grander than the first city. It had a huge tower made of a waste paper basket.

The cities were really very beautiful. Besides all the things I have told of, there were towers and turrets and grand staircases, pagodas and pavilions, canals made bright and water-like by strips of silver paper, and a lake with a boat on it. There were forts filled with toy soldiers.

Philip worked hard and he worked cleverly, and as the cities grew in beauty, he loved them more and more. He was happy now. There was no time to be unhappy in. "I will keep it as it is till Helen comes. How she will love it!" he said.

Finding Raggedy Andy

By Johnny Gruelle

The father of Marcella, who is the owner of Raggedy Ann, is an artist, and sometimes he borrows Raggedy Ann to draw pictures of her for children's books.

ONE DAY, DADDY TOOK Raggedy Ann down to his office and propped her up against some books upon his desk. He wanted to have her where he could see her cheery smile all day.

Daddy wished to catch a whole lot of Raggedy Ann's cheeriness and happiness, and put all this down on paper. Then those who did not have Raggedy Ann dolls might see just how happy a rag doll can be.

So Raggedy Ann stayed at Daddy's studio for three or four days. She was missed very much at home and Marcella longed for her. But she knew that Daddy was borrowing some of Raggedy Ann's sunshine, so she did not complain.

Raggedy Ann did not complain either, for in addition to the sunny, happy smile she always wore (it was painted on) Raggedy Ann had a candy heart, and no one (not even a rag doll) ever complains if they have such happiness about them.

MAGICAL MOMENTS

One evening, just as Daddy was finishing his day's work, a messenger boy came with a package – a nice, soft, lumpy package. Daddy opened it and found a letter.

Grandma had told Daddy, long before this, that at the time Raggedy Ann was made, a neighbour had made a boy doll, Raggedy Andy. She had made him for her little girl, who played with Grandma.

And Grandma told Daddy she had wondered whatever had become of her little playmate and the boy doll, Raggedy Andy.

After reading the letter, Daddy opened the other package, which was inside the nice, soft, lumpy package and found – Raggedy Andy. He had been carefully folded up.

His soft, floppy arms were folded up in front of him, and his soft, floppy legs were folded over his arms. They were held this way by a rubber band.

Raggedy Andy must have wondered why he was being done up this way, but it could not have worried him, for inbetween where his feet came over his face, Daddy saw his cheery smile.

After slipping off the rubber band, Daddy smoothed out the wrinkles in Raggedy Andy's arms and legs. Then he propped Raggedy Ann and Raggedy Andy up against books on his desk, so that they sat facing each other – Raggedy Ann's shoe button eyes looking straight into the shoe button eyes of Raggedy Andy.

They could not speak – not right out before a real person – so they just sat there and smiled at each other.

"So, Raggedy Ann and Raggedy Andy," said Daddy, "I will go away and let you have your visit to yourselves, although it is good to sit and share your happiness by watching you."

Daddy then took the rubber band and placed it around Raggedy Ann's right hand, and around Raggedy Andy's right hand, so that when he had it fixed properly they sat and held each other's hands.

Daddy knew they would wish to tell

each other all the wonderful things that had happened to them since they had parted more than fifty years before.

So, locking his studio door, Daddy left the two rag dolls looking into each other's eyes.

The next morning, when Daddy unlocked his door and looked at his desk, he saw that Raggedy Andy had fallen over so that he lay with his head in the bend of Raggedy Ann's arm.

The Visit to Santa Claus Land

By Anon

JACK AND MARGARET were growing more excited each day, because Christmas was so near. They talked of nothing but Santa Claus.

"Don't you wish you could see him?" they said, over and over.

One night, just before Christmas, Mother

tucked them in bed and left them to go to sleep. But Jack wiggled, Margaret wriggled. At last they both sat up in bed.

"Jack," Margaret whispered, "are you asleep yet?"

"No," said Jack, "I can't go to sleep. Margaret, don't you wish you could see Santa Claus? What's that?"

They both listened, and they heard a little tap, tap on the window. They looked, and there, right in the window, they saw a funny little elf.

"What's that I heard you say? You want to see Santa Claus? Well, I am one of his elves. I am on my way back to Santa Claus Land. I'll take you with me if you really want to go."

Jack and Margaret quickly scrambled from their beds.

"Come on, show us the way!" they cried in great excitement.

"No, indeed," said the elf. "No one must know the way to Santa Claus Land. Kindly wait a moment."

The elf took something soft and thick and dark, and tied it around Jack's eyes. Next he took something soft and thick and dark, and tied it around Margaret's eyes.

"How many fingers before you?" the little elf asked.

Both of them shook their heads. They could not see a wink.

"Very well, now we're off," said the elf.

He took Jack's hand on one side, and

Margaret's on the other. It seemed as if they flew through the window. They went on swiftly for a little while, then the elf whirled them round and round, and off they went again. The children could not tell whether they were going north, south, east or west. After a time they stopped.

"Here we are," said the elf.

He uncovered their eyes and the children saw that they were standing before a big, thick gate.

The elf knocked and the gate swung open. They went through it, right into Santa Claus' garden. There were rows and rows of Christmas trees, all glittering with balls and tinsel, and instead of flower beds there were beds of every kind of toy in the world.

Margaret at once ran over to a bed of dolls.

"Let's see if any of them are ripe," said the elf.

"Ripe?" said Margaret in great surprise.

"Why, of course," said the elf. "Now if this one is ripe it will shut its eyes."

The elf picked a little doll from the bed and laid it in Margaret's arms. Its eyes went half shut and then stuck.

"No, it's not ripe yet," said the elf. "Try this one."

He picked another one, and this one shut its eyes just as if it had gone to sleep.

"We'll take that one," he said, and he dropped it into a big sack he was carrying.

"Come over here, Margaret!" Jack called.

Margaret ran over to another bed and

there were drums – big drums, little drums and middle-sized drums, yellow drums, blue drums, green drums and red drums.

"Can we gather some of these?" said Jack to the elf.

"Of course. Let's see if this one is ripe."

The elf took up a little red drum and gave it a thump with a drum stick. But it made such a strange sound that Jack and Margaret both laughed out loud. The little red drum was put back into the bed and the elf tried another big one. It went Boom! Boom! Boom! Boom! Boom! Jack and Margaret marched along the bed, keeping step to it.

When they had finished picking drums, they went over to a bed filled with horns.

That was the most fun of all. Some of them made very odd noises, and on some the elf played jolly little tunes.

The next bed they came to was filled with toys that could be wound up. There were trains, automobiles, dancing dolls, climbing monkeys, hopping birds, funny wobbling ducks and every kind of toy you could think of. The children stayed at this bed for a long time.

At last Margaret said, "But where is Santa Claus? We wanted to see him."

"Oh, to be sure," said the elf. "Come along," and he led them down a long, winding walk, to the edge of the garden. Then he pointed to a hill in the distance.

"Do you see that large white house?

That is where he lives."

The children stared at it. It was so white that it seemed to shine in the distance.

"Walk right across here," said the elf, "then up the hill to Santa Claus' house."

"Oh, must we walk across there?" said Margaret. She stared down at the deep dark chasm between the garden and the hill. A narrow plank was stretched across it.

"Walk carefully," said the elf, "and mind you don't look down. For if you do, I'm afraid you won't see Santa Claus tonight."

"We'll be very careful," said Jack. "Come along Margaret." He took his little sister's hand and they started across the plank.

They had almost reached the middle of it when Jack looked down.

"Oh!" he said, and gave Margaret a pull. She looked down too, and cried "Oh, Oh!" and down, down, down they went.

Suddenly they landed with a thump. They sat up and rubbed their eyes – they were right in their own beds at home. Mother opened the door.

"Are you awake, children?" she said.

"Oh, Mother, we haven't been asleep. We've been to Santa Claus Land, and we nearly saw Santa Claus!"

Then they told her all about it, and Mother just smiled.

The Dolls' Hospital

An extract from *The Story of Live Dolls*
by Josephine Scribner Gates

Janie is having a magical day. Her dolls have come to life, and now she is peeping out of her gate to see what is happening outside.

SHE WAS JUST IN TIME to see, coming slowly down the street, a white, covered wagon, marked in red letters, "Dolls' Ambulance." It was drawn by six white kittens, who moved along so carefully

58

that Janie decided they must have some very sick patients aboard.

Janie, curious to see what was within, walked around to the back and peeped in at the little open door.

There she saw a sad sight. The wagon was filled with dolls of all sizes, and in such a condition! Arms and legs were off, hair was missing, and some dolls lay with their poor sightless eyes staring up at her, in such a pathetic manner that Janie could hardly keep back the tears.

Each had a trouble. Some told of how their mammas had lost their arms and legs, and how their hair had been off for weeks. Some were sadly neglected, many being wrapped in small bed-quilts and dirty blankets, as they hadn't an outfit to put on.

The dolls told Janie that the Queen of the Dolls had appeared that morning, had gathered them up from their different homes, and was going to take them to a dolls' hospital.

The Queen invited Janie to go with them. Janie ran in to ask her mamma if she could go, and was soon spinning along after them.

They turned into a country road and down a long lane, at the end of which Janie saw a high wall. The Queen told them that the place was called the Doll Farm.

The gate swung open, and when they had all entered, it closed immediately after them. They got out of the ambulance and the Queen led them up a path towards a building with a sign bearing the name:

The Dolls' Hospital

Janie was too much astonished at the sight that met her eyes to follow. All she could see was an orchard of low trees, whose branches hung full of doll clothes, swaying in the cool morning air. There were tiny undergarments and dresses of all colours. She reached out to examine a particularly pretty one, and to see just how it was made, when a voice startled her.

"Don't touch that. It isn't ripe yet."

"Ripe?" said Janie. "Is it growing?"

"Why, of course. Now see. The button holes aren't begun yet, and these buttons aren't near tight enough. It will be about two weeks before that frock can be picked. Now here is one that I can pick tomorrow," and he explained to Janie just how he could tell when it was ready to be removed from the tree.

Then the gardener, for it was he, showed her the trees full of underwear and little petticoats, the bushes of different coloured socks, with shoes and slippers to match, and last of all, the tree of hats. They

were the sweetest things, of many
different shapes, and from the end of
each branch hung bright ribbons
of all colours.

Janie seated herself under a
tree, from whose branches
dainty parasols of all different
colours were dancing and
nodding in the breeze.

"Oh, Mr Gardener, can I
have one please?" He said she
might and asked her which one
she wanted.

"That beautiful one – wait a
moment. They are all so sweet!"
Janie finally decided on the blue – a
beauty with lace and forget-me-nots

63

around the top. The pink one had a wreath of wild roses, and it was hard to give that up, but the blue matched her doll's new dress, and so that decided it. Then the gardener told Janie that she had better go into the hospital and see what they were doing there.

Here Janie found the poor crippled dolls being put in fine shape by little doll nurses, wearing soft grey dresses with white aprons. Legs and arms were being replaced, the blind were made to see with blue eyes and brown, bald heads were covered, and such a wealth of hair did those dolls have – some curly, some braided and with a ribbon, and some hanging straight, for the dolls' mammas to braid or curl as they chose.

When their bodies had finally reached perfection, they went into a bathroom for a bath, and Janie went to help the gardener pick clothes.

Together they wandered about, plucking an outfit for each doll. It was great fun to match the dresses to slippers and stockings, and then to complete the costumes with the proper hats. When they carried the dresses in, what a noise arose! Each doll wanted every dress.

The Queen quieted them and gave clothes to each one, which they soon put on. They looked so sweet, clean and pretty that their own mammas would hardly know them.

When they reached home they found the

yard full of little girls weeping for their lost dolls. But as each doll jumped down and ran to its own mamma, what a chattering and babbling filled the air!

"Who mended you?"

"What lovely hair!"

"Where did you get those clothes?" cried the little girls.

The strange tale that Janie told them of all she had seen, and especially of the clothes growing on trees, seemed too wonderful to be believed, and they envied her such delightful experiences.

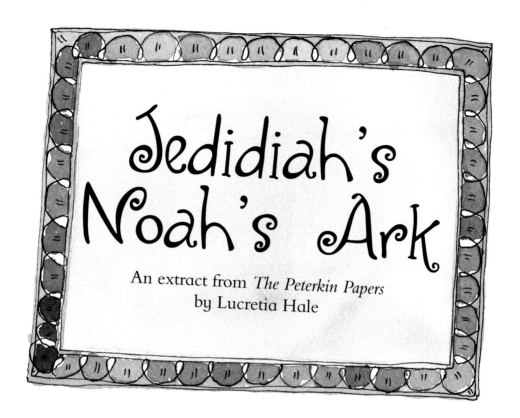

Jedidiah's Noah's Ark

An extract from *The Peterkin Papers*
by Lucretia Hale

*Jedidiah and his family live in the small town of Spinville.
A bandbox was a smart box for keeping hats in.*

IT WAS A MODERATE-SIZED ARK, painted blue, with a slanting roof, held down with a crooked wire. It was brought to Jedidiah one evening, just as he was going to bed, so the crooked wire was not lifted.

Mrs Dyer thought he had better go to bed and get up early to look at his ark.

But Jedidiah could not sleep well, thinking of his ark. It stood by his bedside, and all night long he heard a great racket inside of it. There was a roaring and a grunting and a squeaking – all kinds of strange noises. In the morning he took it downstairs, then lifted the roof.

What a commotion there was inside! The elephant was on the top, the giraffe's long neck was stretched out – one dove flew away directly, and some crows sat on the eaves. The cows were mooing, the cats mewing, the dogs barking, the pigs grunting. Presently, Noah's head appeared

and he looked round for his wife, and then
came Shem and Ham and Japheth with
their wives. They helped out some of the
birds – white, with brown spots – geese and
ducks. Some sly foxes got out by themselves,
leaping from the roof to the back of a
kneeling camel.

Jedidiah's eyes sparkled with joy. At last a great roaring and growling was heard at the bottom of the ark. "It's the wild animals," said Jedidiah.

'If they should get out,' thought Mrs Dyer, 'all the wild tigers and the lions loose in the house!' Mr Dyer stepped up and shut the roof of the ark. It was just in time, for a large bear was standing on his hind legs on the back of a lion, and was looking out. "They ought to have some houses to live in, and barns," said Jedidiah.

In a day or two there was a little village built on a smooth place on the other side of Mr Dyer's house. The minister's daughter had brought a little toy village she had with red roofs. Tom Stubbs built a barn of

wooden bricks for the larger animals, and
Lucy Miles brought a pewter birdcage for
the birds. The elephant knocked out a
brick with his trunk as soon as
he went into the barn, but that
made a good window for
him to look out of.
Jedidiah himself made the
loveliest coop for the
hens, and the boys had a
nice time over a pond
they dug in the mud,
for the ducks.

There was a fence built
around the whole village, high enough to
keep in the elephants and the giraffes,
though they could look over. There was a

bit of pasture-land shut in for the cows, who fell to nibbling as soon as they were put in it. A clover leaf lasted one of the sheep two days. The giraffes found a bush just high enough for them to eat from.

The children were never tired of seeing the camels kneel and rise. They made them carry little burdens – stones that were to be cleared from the field, chips from the henhouse. The townspeople sent a large umbrella, which could be opened over the whole village in case of rain. And, day by day, the people came to look at the wonderful village. There was always something new to see.

One afternoon, Tim Stubbs, in setting up a new pump, gave a knock to the ark, and

sent the whole thing over. The roof snapped
open and out came all the wild beasts. The
hyenas laughed, the lions roared, the bears
growled, and the tigers leapt about to see
whom they could devour.

Noah jumped up on top of the pump, the
elephant knocked out a side of the barn to
see what was the matter, and there was a
general confusion. Tim and Tom Stubbs
declared they would catch the animals, if
Jedidiah would only find something safe to
put them in.

"If we only had a cave!" exclaimed Lucy
Miles, who had hidden herself behind the
kitchen door.

Tim and Tom Stubbs caught one of the
tigers, just as Jedidiah appeared with his

mother's bandbox. They shut the tiger up in the bandbox, then found one of the bears climbing up the pump after Noah. Jedidiah brought a strong string, and tied it to a post. All the rest of the boys ran away at first, but came back and joined in the search for the rest of the beasts.

One of the boys prepared a leash of twine and made a lasso. With this he succeeded in catching the two hyenas. At last the two leopards were found – beautiful creatures, who lashed their tails wildly They were very fierce and wild, and were caught with great difficulty. The leopards were put in the bandbox with the others.

Under a cabbage leaf, fast asleep, the stray tiger was found. There was great delight, for that must be all, surely the ark could have held no more. Lions, tigers, leopards, panthers, lynxes, wildcats – all the animals necessary for a respectable ark, all in twos.

But, oh horror! A jaguar was discovered at the last moment, just before school. One jaguar, and there must be another somewhere. A stray jaguar in Spinville! Noah, his sons and their wives had looked much pleased, but now they shook their heads at seeing only one jaguar.

That a jaguar is loose is the latest news.

The Magic Sled

By John Kendrick Bangs

WHEN JIMMIEBOY woke up the other morning, the ground was white with snow and his heart rejoiced. He had been afraid that the season was going to pass without bringing an opportunity to use the beautiful sled Santa Claus had brought him at Christmas.

The Magic Sled

It was a fine sled, one of the finest he had ever seen. It had a red back, yellow runners and two swan heads standing at the front of it. On the back was painted its name in blue letters, and that name was "Magic".

"Hooray," Jimmieboy cried as he rushed to the window. "Snow at last! Now I can see if Magic can slide."

He dressed hastily — so hastily in fact that he had to undress again, because it was discovered by his mother that he had put his sock on wrong side out, and his left shoe was making his right foot uncomfortable.

"Come along, Magic!" he said, gleefully catching up the rope. And then the left-hand swan head winked its eye at the other swan head and whispered, "Humph! It's plain Jimmieboy doesn't know that we are a magic sled."

"Well, why should he?" returned the other swan head, with a laugh. "He never slid on us."

Jimmieboy was so surprised that he sat down on the sled and was off for – well, where the sled took him. No sooner had he sat down than with a leap that nearly threw him off his balance, the swans started. The steel runners crackled over the snow, and the wind itself was soon left behind.

"Can you swans talk?" Jimmieboy cried, in amazement,

as soon as he could get his breath.

"No, of course not," said the right-hand swan. "It's a queer question for him to ask, isn't it Swanny?"

"Extraordinary, Swayny," said the one on the left. Jimmieboy laughed as, strange to say, this wonderful sled began to slide up a very steep hill.

"Europe!" cried Swayny. "Five minutes for refreshments."

"What do you mean?" said Jimmieboy, as the sled came to a sudden standstill.

"What does any conductor mean when he calls out the name of a station?" said Swayny scornfully. "He means that's where you are at, of course.

79

We've arrived at Europe. We've carried you over the sea in three minutes."

"Really?" cried Jimmieboy.

"Certainly," said Swanny. "You are now in Europe. That blue place you see over on the right is Germany, off to the left is France and that little pink speck is Switzerland. See that glistening thing just on the edge of the pink speck?"

"Yes," said Jimmieboy.

"That's an Alp," said Swanny. "It's too bad we've got to get you home in time for breakfast. If we weren't in such a hurry, we'd let you off so that you could buy an Alp to take home to your brother. You could have snowballs all through the summer if you had an Alp. Ready Swayny?"

"Yes," said Swayny. "All aboard for England!" And then they were off again.

"How did you like Europe Jimmieboy?" asked Swanny.

"Very nice, what I saw of it," said Jimmieboy. "But, of course I couldn't see very much in five minutes."

"Hoh! Hear that, Swayny?" said Swanny. "Couldn't see much in five minutes. Why you could see all Europe in five minutes, if you only looked fast enough. You kept your eye glued on that Alp, I guess."

"That's what he did," said Swayny. "And that's why it was so hard to get the sled started. I had to hump three times before I could get off and it was all because he'd glued his eye on the Alp! Don't do it again,

Jimmieboy. We haven't time to unglue your eye every time we start."

"London!" cried Swanny. That's where they were! Jimmieboy knew it in a minute, because there was a lady coming out of a shop wearing a crown on her head, whom he recognized as the Queen.

"What are you doing here?" the Queen asked.

"I'm sliding until breakfast is ready," he replied.

"But – it is now nearly one o'clock!" said the Queen.

"That's all right, Your Royal Highness," said Swanny. "This is an American boy and it isn't eight o'clock yet where he lives."

"Oh, yes – so it isn't," said the Queen. "I remember now. The sun rises earlier here than it does in America."

"Yes, Ma'am," put in Swayny. "It has to in order to get to America on time."

And before the Queen could say another word, the sled was sliding merrily along at such a rapid pace that Jimmieboy had to throw his arms about Swayny's neck to keep from falling overboard.

"Where are we going to now?" he asked.

"China," said Swanny.

83

"Egypt," said Swayny.

"I said China," cried Swanny, turning his eyes full upon Swayny and glaring at him.

"I know you did," said Swayny. "I may not show 'em, but I have ears. I, on the other hand, said Egypt, and Egypt is where we are going. I want to show Jimmieboy the Pyramids."

"No doubt," said Swanny. "But he's not going to Egypt. Therefore, on to China."

"I'm not going to China, Mr William G. Swanny, and that's all there is to it," said Swayny, angrily.

Whereupon the two strange birds became involved in a dreadful quarrel, one trying to run the sled off towards China, the other trying to steer it over to Egypt. The runners creaked, the red back groaned and finally there came a most dreadful crash. Swanny flew off with his runner to China, and Swayny, freed from his partner, sped on to Egypt.

And Jimmieboy? Well, he fell in between, and by some great good fortune, landed in a heap immediately beside his little bed in his night gown. Out of doors, not a speck of snow was to be seen. Strangest of all, when he was dressed and had gone downstairs, there stood Magic, the two swan heads as spick and span as you please, still waiting to be tried.

The Toys in the Wood

An extract from *The Land of Lost Toys*
by Juliana Horatia Ewing

*A woman, out on a walk, has sat down beneath
a tree she used to play under as a child.*

THE TREE UNDER which I sat was an
old friend. There was a hole at its
base that I knew well. We always used to
say that fairies lived within, but I never saw
anything go in apart from wood beetles.

The Toys in the Wood

There was one going in at that moment.

I had not noticed until then how much larger the hole was than it used to be.

"I suppose the rain and so forth wears it away over time," I said vaguely.

"I suppose it does," said the beetle politely, "will you walk in?"

I don't know why I was not as astonished as you would imagine. I went.

As I stood inside I caught sight of a large spider crouched up in a corner and said, "Can you tell me, sir, if this is Fairyland?"

"Well," he said, "it's a Province. The fact is, it's the Land of Lost Toys. You haven't such a thing as a fly anywhere about you, have you?"

"No," I said, "I'm sorry to say I don't."

I hurried forward, and reached an open space with lights and music. Toys lay in their places looking so incredibly attractive, when all in a moment, a dozen toy fiddles began to play. It was weird fairy music.

When the music began, all the toys rose. The dolls jumped down and began to dance, the puzzles put themselves together, the bricks built houses, the balls flew from side to side, the skipping ropes went round, whilst a go-cart ran

madly about with nobody inside. The beetle
was once more at my elbow.

"There are beautiful toys here," I said.

"Well, yes," he replied, "and some odd-
looking ones too. You see, whatever
has been well used by a child as a
plaything gets a right to come
down here in the end.
Look over there."
I looked, and
said, "It seems to
be a potato."

"So it is," said
the beetle. "It
belonged to an
Irish child in one
of your great cities.

It was the only plaything he ever had. He
played with it every day, until he lost it. No
toys come down here until they are broken
or lost. Look at that box."

"It's my old Toy Box!" I exclaimed.

"You don't mean to say you have any
toys here? If you have, the sooner you make
your way home the better."

"Why?"

"Well," he said, "there's a very strong
feeling in the place. The toys think that they
are ill-treated, and not taken care of by
children in general. And there is some truth
in it. If any of their old masters or mistresses
come this way, they shall be punished."

"How will they be punished?" I asked.

"What they did to their toys, their toys

will do to them."

I turned to go, but somehow I lost the road, so I turned back. As I did so, I heard a click – the lid of a small box burst open and up jumped a figure. He was very like my old Jack-in-a-box. My back began to creep, and I tried to remember whether it were my brother or I who came up with the idea of making a small bonfire, and burning the old Jack-in-a-box. At this moment he nodded to me and spoke.

"Oh! It's you, is it?" he said.

"No, it's not," I answered hastily.

"Who is it, then?" he inquired.

"I'm sure I don't know," I said, and really I was so confused that I hardly did.

"Well, we know," said the Jack-in-a-box,

"and that's all that's needed. Now, my friends," he continued, to the toys who had begun to crowd round us, "the hour of our revenge has come."

What was that familiar figure among the rest, in a yellow silk dress? It was my dear doll Rosa. No one could say I had ill-treated her. She fixed her eyes on me with a smile.

"Take notice," shouted the Jack-in-a-box, "that the rule of this court is tit for tat."

"Tie a string round her neck and take her out bathing in the brooks," I heard a voice say. It was my old Dowager Doll.

"It's not fair," I said,

92

"the string was only to keep you from being carried away by the stream."

"Tear her hair off," shrieked the Dowager. "Flatten her nose!"

A dozen voices shouted for a dozen different punishments, and terrible suggestions were made, which I have forgotten now. I have a vague idea that several voices cried that I was to be sent to be washed in somebody's pocket, and that through all the din the thick voice of my old leather ball repeated,

"Throw her into the dustbin."

Suddenly Rosa spoke up. "My dears," she began, "Let us follow our usual rule. I claim the first turn because I was the prisoner's oldest toy."

"She is right," said the Jack-in-a-box. "The prisoner is delivered into the hands of our trusty and well-beloved Rosa – doll of the first class – for punishment according to the strict law of tit for tat."

I suddenly found myself walking away with my hand in Rosa's. Under one of the big trees Rosa made me sit down, propping me against the trunk as if I should otherwise have fallen, and a box of tea cups came tumbling up to our feet.

"Take a little tea, my love," said Rosa,

pressing a teacup to my lips.

"What are you doing?" roared the Jack-in-a-box at this moment. "You are not punishing her!"

"I am treating her as she treated me," answered Rosa. "I believe that tit for tat is the rule, and that at present it is my turn."

I thanked her gratefully.

"I think you shall go to bed now, dear," she said. And, taking my hand once more, she led me to a big doll's bed.

"You are very kind," I said, "but I am not tired and it will not bear my weight."

"Well, if you will not go to bed I must put you there," said Rosa, and she snatched me up in her arms and laid me down.

Of course it was just as I expected. I had

hardly touched the two little pillows when
the woodwork gave way with a crash, and I
fell – fell – fell –

As soon as I could, I sat up and felt
myself all over. A little stiff, but, as it seemed,
unhurt. Oddly enough, I found that I was
back under the old tree in the little wood.

Was it all a dream? The toys had vanished, the lights were out, the evening was chilly, and the hole no larger than it was thirty years ago.

I have returned to the spot many times since, but I have never been able to repeat my visit to the Land of Lost Toys.

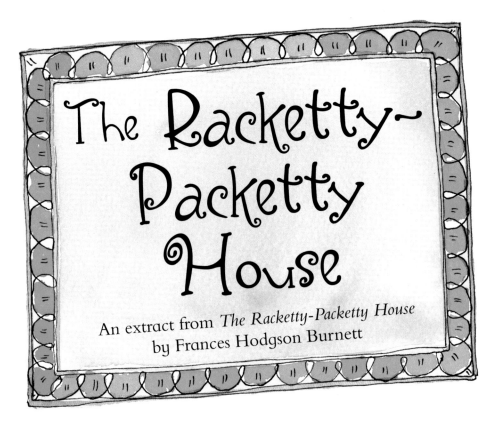

The Racketty-Packetty House

An extract from *The Racketty-Packetty House*
by Frances Hodgson Burnett

*This is a Victorian story about a doll's house. In those days,
rich people had a servant called a nurse to look after the children,
and the children's room was called a nursery.*

RACKETTY-PACKETTY HOUSE was in a corner of Cynthia's nursery. It had been pushed there to be out of the way when Tidy Castle was brought in, on Cynthia's birthday. The minute she saw it she called out, "Oh! What a beautiful doll castle! What shall we do with that untidy old Racketty-Packetty House now?"

It had always been called The Dolls' House before, but ever afterwards – when it was spoken of at all – it was just called Racketty-Packetty House.

Tidy Castle was grand and new and modern, and Racketty-Packetty House was as old-fashioned as it could be. It had belonged to Cynthia's Grandmamma, and had been made in the days when Queen Victoria was a little girl. When she was given it, Cynthia's Grandmamma had clapped her hands, and taken the dolls out and given each one of them a grand name.

"This one shall be Amelia," she said.

"This one is Charlotte, this is Victoria Leopoldina, this one Aurelia Matilda, this one Leontine, and this one Clotilda. These boys shall be Augustus and Rowland and Vincent and Charles Edward Stuart."

For a long time they had parties and balls. They went to royal weddings and were married themselves, and had families and every luxury. But that was long, long ago, and now all was changed.

Their house had grown shabbier and shabbier, and their clothes had grown simply awful. Aurelia Matilda and Victoria Leopoldina had been broken and thrown into the dustbin, and Leontine had had nearly all her paint licked off by a puppy. As for the boys, Rowland and Vincent had disappeared. The only ones who were left were Clotilda, Amelia, Charlotte, Leontine, Augustus and Charles Edward Stuart. They even had their names changed.

After Leontine had had her paint licked off, Cynthia had called her Ridiklis. Charlotte and Amelia, Cynthia had called Meg and Peg, Clotilda she called Kilmanskeg, Augustus she called Gustibus, and Charles Edward Stuart was Peter Piper. So that was the end of their grand names.

However, you never saw a family have such fun. They could make up stories and pretend things and invent games out of nothing. Everything was as happy as it could be until Tidy Castle came, and then the whole family had rather a fright.

It happened in this way. When the dolls' house was lifted by the nurse and carried into the corner behind the door, of course it was rather an exciting and shaky thing for Meg, Peg, Kilmanskeg, Gustibus and Peter Piper (Ridiklis was out shopping). The furniture tumbled about and everybody had to hold on to anything they could catch hold of. When the nurse sat their house down on the floor with a bump, they all got up and ran to peep out of the windows.

It was just at this minute that Ridiklis came back. The nurse had found her under a chair and stuck her in through a window. "Good gracious, if you knew what I have just heard!" she said. "When Cynthia asked what she should do with this old Racketty-Packetty House, the nurse said, 'Oh! I'll put it behind the door for the present and then it shall be carried downstairs and burned.'"

"Oh!" cried out Peter Piper.

"Oh!" said Gustibus.

"Oh! Oh! Oh!" said Meg and Peg and Kilmanskeg. Peter Piper sat down.

"I don't care how shabby it is," he said. "It's a jolly nice place and it's the only house we've ever had."

There is no knowing what would have happened to them if Peter Piper hadn't heard something.

"I say," he said, "do you hear that noise?"
They all listened and heard a rumbling.
Peter Piper ran to the window and then ran
back, grinning.

"It's the nurse rolling the armchair before
the house to hide it. Hooray! If they don't
see us they will forget all about us, and we
shall not be burned up at all."

It certainly seemed as if they were quite
safe for some time at least. The big chair hid
them, and both the nurse and Cynthia
seemed to forget that there was such a thing
as a Racketty-Packetty House. Cynthia was
so delighted with Tidy Castle that she
played with nothing else for days and days.

The Tidy Castle dolls were grand beyond
words, and they were all lords and ladies.

There was Lady Gwendolen Vere de Vere,
Lady Muriel Vere de Vere and Lady Doris.
And there was Lord Hubert and Lord
Rupert and Lord Francis, who were all
handsome enough to make you feel as if
you could faint. And there was their mother,
the Duchess of Tidyshire, and of course
there were all sorts of maids and cooks.

"It's almost like being grand ourselves,
just to be able to watch them," said Meg
and Peg and Kilmanskeg, flattening their
noses against the attic windows.

They could see bits of the white and gold
drawing room, with the Duchess sitting
reading near the fire, and Lady Gwendolen
playing upon the harp.

"Isn't it fun," said Peter Piper. He turned

three somersaults in the middle of the room, then stood on his head and wiggled his toes. They shouted so much with laughing that Ridiklis ran in with a saucepan, because she was cooking turnips.

"You mustn't laugh so loud," she cried out. "The Tidy Castle people will begin to complain."

"Oh! Scrump!" exclaimed Peter Piper. He often invented dolls' slang.

"They are going to have a dinner of ten courses," sighed Ridiklis. "I can see them cooking it. And I have nothing but turnips to give you."

106

"Who cares!" said Peter Piper. "Let's have ten courses of turnips and pretend each course is like the one they are having at Tidy Castle."

"I like turnips almost better than anything," said Gustibus. "I can eat ten courses of turnips like a shot."

So they divided their turnips into ten courses. Peter Piper kept pretending he was a butler, and announced the names of the dishes in such a grand way that they all laughed, and said that they would rather watch the Tidy Castle people than be the Tidy Castle people themselves.

Children and their Toys

109

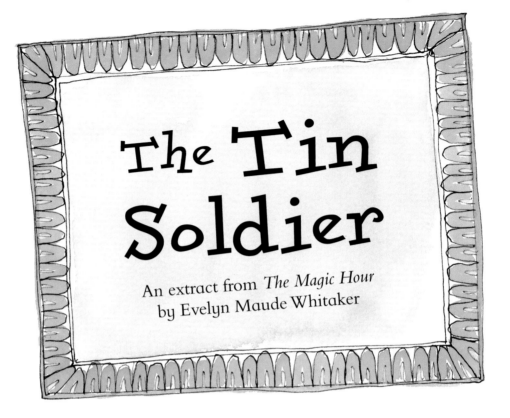

The Tin Soldier

An extract from *The Magic Hour*
by Evelyn Maude Whitaker

*Flossie has found a way to make one toy come to life every night
when she is in bed. A 'Tommy' is an old name for a soldier.*

FLOSSIE PULLED OUT a box from under
her bed. She leaned out and peered
down at the muddle of old scrappy things
that were in it – a pencil box, some marbles,
a tiny teapot, a ball, some bricks, a few

110

tiddlywinks, a whistle and a tin soldier.

Flossie stretched down and picked up the battered little warrior. She stood him in front of her and, for a moment or two, she was very thoughtful.

"Yes, I've decided," she said suddenly. "I'll bring the soldier to life and see what he has to tell me." Exactly half a minute later, the old tin soldier moved his head sharply.

"Hooray!" Flossie said aloud. "It's rather jolly having a real live Tommy on my bed."

The little man turned on her so suddenly and shouted so fiercely that she nearly knocked him over.

"My name isn't Tommy and I'll thank you to stop feeling jolly. There's nothing to be jolly about."

111

Flossie looked at him in surprise.

"What do you mean?" she asked, after a moment's silence.

"What I say," snapped the soldier.

Well, it was very bad-tempered of him to snap at her so, but Flossie took no notice and went on talking. "You see, my brother has gone to boarding school," she said. "Most of his soldiers are in the drawer, but somehow you have got into that box."

"Then why couldn't you leave me

there?" asked the soldier in a harsh voice.

"I'm beginning to wish that I had," Flossie answered. "What's the matter?"

"I don't suppose you'd understand half of what I would say," the soldier replied.

"Oh! I think I should. You see, we learn all about battles at school."

The tin soldier looked rather pleased at that. He gave a very tiny smile.

"I'm very glad you learn something that sensible," he said at last.

"Do you like battles?" Flossie asked.

"Love them," he answered, "except when I'm an enemy."

"An enemy! How do you mean?"

"When I'm one of the enemy, I'm all the time being knocked over and pushed about

113

and treated roughly. I never get a chance to stand grandly in a row, or head a file of marching troops, and that's what I like best. No one wants to be the enemy, but, of course, some of us have to be, or there couldn't be a battle. But, you see, it's so horrid because you never win. Boys always make the enemy lose – in the end they are always beaten."

"How funny!" Flossie said. "I've often watched my brother playing with you, but I never thought of that. Of course, you are not often an enemy, are you?"

The little soldier leaned forward and looked into her face.

"It's a dreadful thing," he said in a solemn voice, "but the last five times that we

114

have been out, I've been one of the enemy."

"I wonder how that has happened," exclaimed Flossie.

"I've thought and thought," the soldier answered, "and the only reason that I can think of is that I'm a bit old and battered. You'll notice that my paint is off in several places, and I think Stephen very often has the shabbiest soldiers for the enemy. It worries me dreadfully."

His voice trailed away into a piteous little squeak, and Flossie leaned forward, looking at him carefully.

Yes, it was so! She could hardly believe her eyes, but it was so. It was so tiny that she could only just be sure that a tiny tear was slowly falling from the tin soldier's eye.

115

She put out a finger and gently patted the little man on the arm.

"You see," he said hopelessly, "I am rather battered and shabby, and now that I've been thrown into the odds and ends box, I shall never get back into the regiment. I'm almost certain to be thrown away before Stephen comes back from school. I shouldn't mind so much, if I hadn't been an enemy in my last five battles, but as it is—"

He made a little choking sound, and Flossie was so afraid that he was going to cry again, that she said hurriedly, "Oh! Don't make yourself unhappy. I'm sure I can help you."

"But how?" asked the soldier. "How can

you help me?"

"I'll tell you," she began happily. "I think
I can make nearly everything come right
for you again."

"But how? But how?" shouted the tin
soldier, his face growing happy with hope.

"Well, first, after you have stopped being
alive, I'll get my paint box and carefully
make you look nice and new again."

"But will the paint stick on all right?"

"Yes, because I have some oil paints of
Dad's. I can make you look ever so grand
and I'll do it very nicely. When I have done
that, and you are dry and ever so fine, I'll
put you carefully back with the other
soldiers in Stephen's drawer. You will look so
fresh and new that, when he comes home,

he'll never dream of making you one of the enemy. There!"

Flossie smiled happily, and a shrill little laugh from the soldier rang through the air. "Ha! Ha! Ha! Oh! That's just fine," he said. "I'm sorry I was cross. Ha! Ha! Ha!"

He drew himself up to attention and suddenly marched forward, shouting, "Left, right, left, right." The tin soldier was going at such a rate that, before Flossie could put out a hand to stop him, he had marched right off the bed and fallen headlong onto the carpet.

She leaned over and picked him up.

"Oh! I do hope you haven't hurt yourself," she said.

The tin soldier did not answer, and Flossie looked at him closely.

"I do hope," she began again, and then stopped. His 'alive' time had ended – the tin soldier was only a little toy once more. Flossie was sorry, but glad that he had understood that everything was going to be right again.

'I shall bring the paints,' she thought, 'and, when he is dry, I'll put him back with the others.'

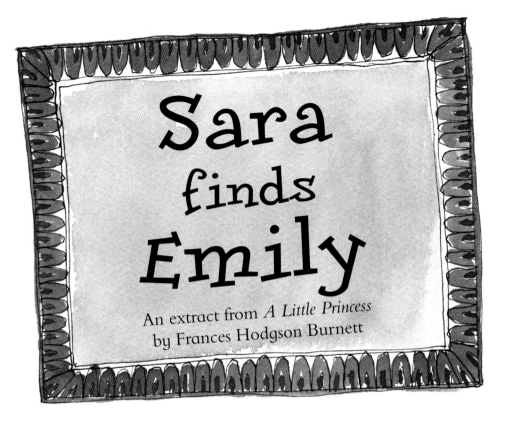

Sara finds Emily

An extract from *A Little Princess*
by Frances Hodgson Burnett

*Sara Crewe is being sent to a boarding school in London,
run by a woman called Miss Minchin, while her father,
Captain Crewe, goes to India.*

"**I AM NOT IN THE LEAST** anxious about her education," Captain Crewe said, as he held Sara's hand and patted it. "The difficulty will be to keep her from learning too fast and too much. She is always sitting with her little nose burrowing into books. Drag her away from her books when she reads too much. Make her ride her pony or go out and buy a new doll. She ought to play more with dolls."

"Papa," said Sara, "if I went out and bought a new doll every few days, I should have more than I could be fond of. Dolls ought to be friends. Emily is going to be my friend."

Captain Crewe looked at Miss Minchin, and Miss Minchin looked back at him.

"Who is Emily?" Miss Minchin inquired.

"Tell her, Sara," Captain Crewe said, smiling at her.

Sara's green-grey eyes looked very solemn and quite soft as she answered.

"She is a doll I haven't got yet," she said. "She is a doll Papa is going to buy for me. We are going out together to find her. I have called her Emily. She is going to be my friend when Papa is gone. I want her to talk to about him."

Miss Minchin's large smile became very flattering indeed.

"What an original child!" she said. "What a darling little creature!"

"Yes," said Captain Crewe, drawing Sara close. "She is a darling little creature. Take great care of her for me, Miss Minchin."

Sara stayed with her father at his hotel for several days, in fact, she remained with him until he sailed away to India. They went out and visited many big shops

together, and at last they found Emily. But
they went to a number of toy shops and
looked at a great many dolls before they
discovered her.

"I want her to look as if she wasn't a
doll really," Sara said. "I want her to look
as if she listens when I talk to her. The
trouble with dolls, Papa" – and she put her
head on one side and reflected as she said
it – "the trouble with dolls is that they never
seem to hear."

So they looked at big ones and little
ones, at dolls with black eyes and dolls with
blue, at dolls with brown curls and dolls
with golden braids, and at dolls dressed and
dolls undressed.

After a number of disappointments they

decided to walk and look in at the shop
windows, and let the cab follow them. They
had passed two or three places without even
going in, when, as they were approaching a
shop that was really not a very large one,
Sara suddenly started and clutched her
father's arm.

"Oh, Papa!" she cried. "There is Emily!"

There was an expression in her green-
grey eyes as if she had just recognized
someone she was fond of.

"She is actually waiting there for us!" she
said. "Let us go in to her."

"Dear me," said Captain Crewe, "I feel
as if we ought to have someone to
introduce us."

"You must introduce me and I will

introduce you," said Sara. "But I knew her the minute I saw her, so perhaps she knew me, too."

Perhaps she had known her. The doll certainly had a very intelligent expression in her eyes when Sara took her in her arms. She was a large doll, but not too large to carry about easily. She had naturally curling golden-brown hair, which hung like a mantle about her, and her eyes were a deep, clear, grey-blue, with soft, thick eyelashes, which were real eyelashes and not mere painted lines.

"Of course," said Sara, looking into her face as she held her on her knee, "of course Papa, this is Emily."

So Emily was bought and actually taken

to a children's outfitter's shop, and measured for a wardrobe as grand as Sara's own. She had lace frocks, and velvet and muslin ones, and hats and coats and beautiful lace-trimmed underclothes, and gloves and handkerchiefs and furs.

"I should like her always to look as if she was a child with a good mother," said Sara. "I'm her mother, though I am going to make a companion of her."

Captain Crewe would really have enjoyed the shopping tremendously, but a sad thought kept tugging at his heart. He got out of his bed in the middle of that night, and went and stood looking down at Sara, who lay asleep with Emily in her arms. Her black hair was spread out on the pillow, and Emily's golden-brown hair mingled with it. Both of them had lace-ruffled nightgowns, and both had long eyelashes that lay and curled up on their cheeks. Emily looked so like a real child that Captain Crewe felt glad she was there. He drew a big sigh.

"Heigh-ho, little Sara," he said to himself. "I don't believe you know how much your daddy will miss you."

The next day Captain Crewe took Sara to Miss Minchin's. He was to sail away the next morning. Captain Crewe went with Sara into her sitting room, and they bade each other goodbye. Sara sat on his knee and held the lapels of his coat in her small hands. She looked long and hard at his face.

128

Sara finds Emily

"Are you learning me by heart, little Sara?" he said, stroking her hair.

"No," she answered. "I know you by heart. You are inside my heart." And they hugged tightly as if they would never let each other go.

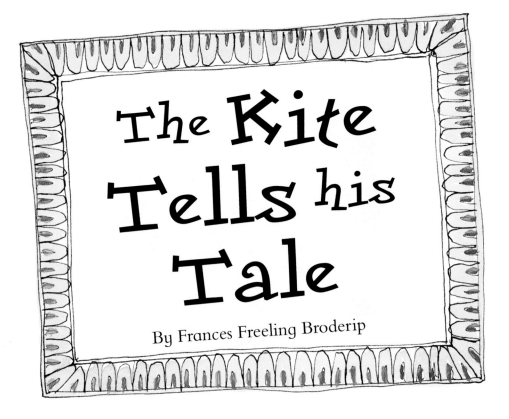

The Kite Tells his Tale

By Frances Freeling Broderip

AT TEATIME, one summer evening,
Mamma said to the children,
"Tomorrow Uncle Gee is coming!" They all
burst out in one shout of delight, for Uncle
Gee was their favourite uncle, and always
ready for fun and games.

130

The Kite Tells his Tale

And the next day, Uncle Gee came, to the great delight of the children. But, to their horror, they looked out and saw the sky covered with clouds, and heard the steady, heavy drops of rain falling.

"What a nuisance," growled Bob and Tom, "when Uncle Gee promised to have a game of cricket with us!"

"O dear," said Mary, "and I wanted to show him the new hammock swing!"

"Rain, rain, go to Spain," chanted Baby.

"What's the matter now?" said Uncle Gee, coming in. "All this racket about a little rain! Why, I was just thinking what a day it would be to make a kite!"

"Make a kite!" shouted Bob. "Oh Uncle Gee, can you show us how to do it?"

"I think I can, Bob," replied his uncle. And when breakfast was over, to work they all went. Papa found some slips of light thin wood and lent his best knife. Mamma gave some beautiful white material to cover the frame with, and her glue pot as well. Uncle Gee soon had the long table covered with all sorts of things and had set everybody to work.

"Now," said Uncle Gee, "Mary, you and Jeanie can find me some strips of coloured paper for the tail, and Dora, you get me a long ball of string."

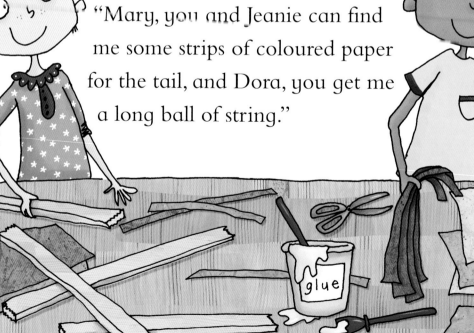

The Kite Tells his Tale

And so the work went on, Bob and Tom helping Uncle Gee, and Mary and Jeanie supplying the long piece of string, provided for the tail, with its cross pieces of paper to serve as light weights. They busily snipped some fine red paper in order to make a grand tassel to finish the tail with.

"The kite is getting beautifully dry and tight," said Uncle Gee, as he took his place at dinner. "What shall we make it? A flying dragon, like the Chinese flags and lanterns?"

"Oh yes! Uncle Gee," cried Dora, "do make it a dragon – a green dragon with a fiery tail!"

"A fairy with wings," suggested Mary, "with a star on her forehead."

"Or a ship," said Jeanie. "A ship with masts and sails painted for her, because you know she does sail through the air, Uncle Gee!"

"Paint it like a daisy," said Baby, "or make buttercups all over it!"

"Well, we'll see," said Uncle Gee. "When dinner is over we'll have a solemn council on the matter, and the most votes shall carry the day."

After dinner, they found the great kite very dry, and nice and flat it was too. They were all delighted with it.

"Now," said Uncle Gee, "once and for all

134

what is it to be? A ship, a dragon or what? It is to be put to the vote – what do you say?"

And so there was a great deal of talking and chattering among them all, and at last the children agreed to ask Uncle Gee to make the kite a bird.

"But we can't settle what kind of bird it is to be," said Bob. "I wanted an eagle, but Tom liked an owl better, and Mary said she liked a dove, while Jeanie said it must be a peacock. Dora wanted a swan, and Baby bawled out for a robin! So you must decide out of all the number, Uncle Gee."

"All right," was Uncle Gee's reply, and to work he went. He painted away while the children all looked on and made remarks as he sketched in the outline. But they began

135

to press round him, so Uncle Gee declared
he would not do another stroke till they left
him alone. So off they went to the other
end of the table, and got the tail in order.

By the time that the tail was finished,
Uncle Gee had completed the kite. Turning
it round to the children, he showed a bird of
such a kind as had never been
seen before! It had the head of
an owl, with its great staring
eyes, the broad wings of an
eagle, the neck of a dove,
the breast of a robin, the
many-eyed tail of a
peacock, and the
yellow webbed
feet of a swan!

The Kite Tells his Tale

The children gazed at it for a moment in utter surprise, and then they all burst into shouts of approval.

"There," said Uncle Gee, "I hope I have satisfied you all. I am sure such a bird as this would make its fortune in a zoo!"

"Oh! What a jolly fellow!" shouted Bob and Tom, clapping their hands, while the girls danced round quite delighted.

"Now," said Uncle Gee, "I think tomorrow will be a fine day after the rain, and we shall be able to make this fine fellow fly."

So they tied on my tail and made me thoroughly ready for the next morning's cruise. Then they all went to bed the happiest set of little ones within fifty miles around.

Many a flight I had with them over field, meadow and moor, and many a tree have I got entangled with. At last, Bob became quite expert at climbing trees, and all owing to the practise he had in getting me.

So here you have an end of my history, which contains, as you see now, no flying adventures at all. If I had time, I could tell you of many curious things I saw in my airy flights, and some about the clouds I went so near, but I must leave that until another day.

138

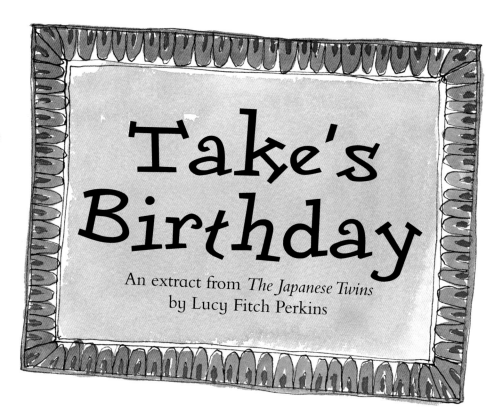

Take's Birthday

An extract from *The Japanese Twins*
by Lucy Fitch Perkins

Taro and Take are boy and girl twins who live in Japan.
This story shows Take following the old custom of celebrating
the Japanese festival of 'girls' day' as if it was her birthday.
A kimono is a Japanese dress, and 'sayonara' means 'goodbye'.

TARO AND TAKE loved their birthdays the best of all the days in the year. They had two of them. Most twins have only one birthday between them, but Japanese twins have two. That is because all

139

the boys in Japan celebrate their birthdays together on one day, and all the girls celebrate theirs together on another day.

Take's birthday came first. One morning, when she woke up, Take said excitedly, "Only six days more."

The next morning she said, "Only five days more." One morning she jumped out of bed very early and said, "Oh, it's today! Today! It begins this very minute."

Before breakfast, Take's father reached up to the high shelf and brought down the big red box that held the dolls. It was as big as a trunk. Then he reached down another box and carried them both into the house.

Although it was so early in the morning, Take's mother had already put fresh flowers

in the vase, in honour of Take's birthday.
The bedding had been put away, and on
one side of the room there were five shelves,
like steps against the wall. Take knew what
they were for.

"Oh," she said, "everything is all ready to
begin! May I open the boxes right now?"

Her mother said, "Yes."

They opened the red box first. It was
full of dolls. A whole trunkful of dolls!
Thirty-five of them!

The first doll Take took out was a very
grand lady doll, dressed in stiff silk robes,
embroidered with chrysanthemums.

"Here's the Empress," Take cried, as she
set the Empress doll up against the trunk.
Then she ran to get her dear everyday doll.

Take called her everyday doll Morning
Glory, sometimes just Glory for short. Glory
was still asleep in Take's bed.

Take took Glory to the
trunk and put her down on her knees
before the Empress. "Make your bow," she
said. Glory bowed so low that she fell over
on her nose!

Take reached into the box and carefully

lifted out the Emperor doll, who was dressed
in stiff silk, too. He sat up straight against
the trunk, beside the Empress. Take made
Glory bow to the Emperor. This time Glory
didn't fall on her nose.

These dolls had belonged to Take's
grandmother. She had played with them on
her birthdays, and then Take's mother had
played with them on her birthdays. Still
they were not broken or torn – they had
been so well cared for.

The dolls were taken out only once
in the whole year, and that time was called
the Feast of Dolls.

Take's mother had covered the five steps
with a beautiful piece of silk. Take placed
the Emperor and Empress in the middle of

143

the top step. Then she ran back to the trunk
to get more dolls.

There were girl dolls, and boy dolls, and
lady dolls in beautiful dresses, and baby
dolls in little kimonos, strapped to the backs
of bigger dolls.

Take took every doll to the steps. She
made each one bow very low before the
Emperor and Empress, then she put him in
his own place. All the shelves were filled so
full that one baby doll spilled over the edge
and fell on the floor!

Then Take opened the other box. She
took out a little stove, some blue-and-white
doll dishes and two tiny lacquered tables.
While she was taking out these things, her
father brought in a new box that she had

never seen before. He put it down on the
floor before the steps. Take was so busy she
didn't see it at first. When she did, she
shouted, "Oh, Father, is it for me?"

"Yes, it is for you," Take's father said.

"Oh, thank you, whatever it is!" said Take.

She flew to the box and untied the string.
When she lifted the cover, there was a
beautiful, big toy house, made almost like
the house the twins lived in! It had a porch
and sliding screens, and a cupboard with
doll bedding in it. The toy house even had
an alcove with a little vase in it. There was
a flower in the vase! There were little straw
mats on the floor!

Take lifted the mats and slid the screens
back and forth. She put her little stove in

the kitchen. Take was too happy for words, and ran to her father saying, "Thank you, ten thousand times, dear Father."

Just then Taro came in, rubbing his eyes. He was still sleepy.

"Oh, Taro," cried Take, "look at my new toy house!"

Now Taro didn't think much of dolls, but he liked the big toy house just as much as Take did.

"I know what I'll do. I'll make you a little garden for your house," he said.

"Oh, that will be beautiful!" cried Take.

Taro found a box cover and filled it with sand. He set a little bowl in the sand and filled it with water, for a pond. Then he broke off little bits of branches and twigs,

146

and stuck them up in the sand for trees. Taro
made a tiny mountain like the one in their
garden. He put a little bridge over the pond
and bright pebbles around it.

When the garden was all finished, the
twins put it down beside the toy house.
Then they put Glory in the garden, beside
the tiny pond.

Just as Take was wiping Glory's face, her
mother came in dressed for the street. Take
had put on one of her gayest kimonos that
morning, because it was her birthday, so she
was all ready to go. Her mother helped her
strap Glory onto her back, and the two
started down the street.

There were other mothers and other little
girls with dolls on their backs in the street,

147

too. They were all going to one place – the doll shop! Each little girl had some money to buy a new doll.

Such chattering and laughing and talking you never heard! And such gay little dresses you never saw, nor such happy smiling faces.

At the doll shop there were rows and rows of dolls, and swarms and swarms of little girls looking at them. Take saw a roly-poly baby doll, with a funny tuft of black hair on his head.

"This is the one I want, if you please," she said to the shopkeeper, and gave him her money.

"Glory," she said over her shoulder, "this is your new little brother."

Take's Birthday

Taro had had fun all afternoon with the garden. He had made a little well to put in it out of boxes.

Then the twins' mother brought out some sweet rice cakes. The maids brought out tiny tables and set them around. Take brought a doll's teapot and placed it with

toy cups on her little table. Then she made
real tea and they had a party. For candy
they had sugared beans and peas. They
gave some of everything to the dolls. Take
sat up just as late as she wanted to that
night. It was eight o'clock when she went to
bed. She hugged each one of the thirty-five
dolls when she said good night to them.

"Sayonara, Sayonara," she said to each
one. "Goodbye for a whole year, you
darling dolls."

Then she took her dear old Glory and
went happily to bed.

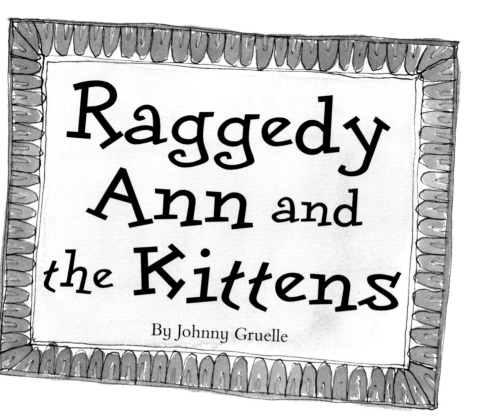

Raggedy Ann and the Kittens

By Johnny Gruelle

*Marcella owns a whole set of toys, including a soldier doll,
Uncle Clem, two tiny dolls called penny dolls, and her beloved
rag doll called Raggedy Ann. Fido is her dog.*

MARCELLA HAD COME EARLY in the morning and dressed all the dolls and placed them about the nursery. Some of the dolls had been put in the little red chairs around the little doll table.

CHILDREN AND THEIR TOYS

There was nothing to eat upon the table except a turkey, a fried egg and an apple, all painted in natural colours. The little teapot and other doll dishes were empty, but Marcella had told them to enjoy their dinner while she was away.

The French doll had been given a seat upon the doll sofa and Uncle Clem had been placed at the piano. Marcella picked up Raggedy Ann and carried her out of the nursery when she left, telling the dolls to "be real good children."

When the door closed, the tin soldier winked at the Dutch-boy doll.

"Shall I play you a tune?" Uncle Clem asked the French doll.

At this all the dolls laughed, for Uncle

152

Clem could not play any tune. Raggedy Ann was the only doll who had ever taken lessons, and she could play 'Peter Peter Pumpkin Eater' with one hand. In fact, Marcella had almost worn out Raggedy Ann's right hand teaching it to her!

"Yes, play something lively!" said the French doll.

So Uncle Clem began hammering the eight keys on the toy piano with all his might. But then, a noise was suddenly heard upon the stairs.

Quick as a wink, all the dolls took the same positions in which they had been placed by Marcella that morning, for they did not wish people to know that they could move about.

But it was only Fido. He put his nose in the door and looked around.

All the dolls at the table looked steadily at the painted food. Uncle Clem leaned upon the piano keys, looking just like he had when he had been placed there.

"I've found something I must tell Raggedy Ann about," Fido said excitedly. "It's kittens!"

"How lovely!" cried all the dolls. "Real live kittens?"

"Real live kittens!" replied Fido. "Three little tiny ones, out in the barn!"

"Oh, I wish Raggedy Ann was here,"

cried the French doll. "She would know what to do about it."

"That's why I wanted to see her," said Fido. "I did not know there were any kittens and I went into the barn to hunt for mice. The first thing I knew, Mamma Cat came bouncing right at me with her eyes looking green! I knew there must be something inside or she would not have jumped at me that way," Fido continued. "And what was my surprise to find three tiny little kittens in an old basket, way back in a dark corner."

"Go get them, Fido, and bring them up so we can see them," said the tin soldier.

"Not me!" said Fido. "If I had a suit of tin clothes on like you have I might do it, but you know cats can scratch very hard."

155

"We will tell Raggedy Ann when she comes in," said the French doll.

So when Raggedy Ann had been returned to the nursery, the dolls could hardly wait until Marcella had put on their nighties and left them for the night. Then they quickly told Raggedy Ann all about the kittens.

Raggedy Ann suggested that all the dolls go out to the barn and see the kittens. This they did easily, for the window was open and it was but a short jump to the ground.

They found Fido out near the barn, watching a hole.

"I was afraid something might disturb them," he said, "for Mamma Cat went away about an hour ago."

Raggedy Ann and *the* Kittens

All the dolls, with Raggedy Ann in the lead, crawled through the hole and ran to the basket.

Just as Raggedy Ann started to pick up one of the kittens, there was a lot of howling and yelping, and Fido came bounding through the hole, with Mamma Cat behind him.

"I'm surprised at you, Mamma Cat," said Raggedy Ann. "Fido has been watching your kittens for an hour while you were away. He would not hurt them for anything."

"I'm sorry, then," said Mamma Cat.

"Have you told the folks up at the house about your kittens?" Raggedy Ann asked.

"Oh my, no!" exclaimed Mamma Cat.

"At the last place I lived the people found out about my kittens and do you know, all the kittens disappeared!"

"But all the folks at this house are very kind people and would love your kittens," cried all the dolls.

"Let's take them right up to the nursery," said Raggedy Ann, "and Mistress can find them there in the morning."

"How lovely!" said all the dolls in chorus. "Do, Mamma Cat!"

So after a great deal of persuasion, Mamma Cat finally agreed. Raggedy Ann took two of the kittens and carried them to the house, while Mamma Cat carried the other.

Raggedy Ann wanted to give the kittens

her bed, but Fido insisted that Mamma Cat and the kittens should have his soft basket.

The dolls could hardly sleep that night, they were so anxious to see what Mistress would say when she found the dear little kittens in the morning.

When Marcella came to the nursery, the first thing she saw was the three little kittens. She cried out in delight and carried them all down to show to Mamma and Daddy. They said the kittens could stay in the nursery and belong to Marcella.

Marcella finally decided upon three names – Prince Charming for the white kitten, Cinderella for the tabby, and Princess Golden for the kitten with yellow stripes.

So that is how the three little kittens

160

came to live in the nursery. And Mamma
Cat found out that Fido was a very good
friend, too. She grew to trust him so much
she would even let him help to wash the
kittens' faces!

A Family Christmas

An extract from *What Katy Did* by Susan Coolidge

*Katy Carr has hurt her back and has to stay in bed,
but her brothers and sisters always try to make her part of the fun.
She is talking about Christmas plans for the children with
her aunt, who looks after her.*

"**I THOUGHT OF** such a nice plan
yesterday," Katy said. "It was that all of
them should hang their stockings up here
tomorrow night instead of in the nursery.
Then I could see them open their presents,

you know. Could they, Aunt Izzie? It would be real fun."

"I don't believe there will be any objection," replied her aunt. She looked as if she were trying not to laugh. Katy wondered what was the matter with her.

"I wish I had something pretty for everybody," Katy went on, wistfully. "There's my pink sash," she said suddenly. "I might give that to Clover. Would you please fetch it and let me see, Aunt Izzie? It's in the top drawer."

Aunt Izzie brought the sash. It proved to be quite fresh.

"I wish I had something nice for Elsie. What she wants most of all is a writing desk," Katy said. "And Johnnie wants a sled.

But, oh dear! These are such big things. And I've only got two dollars and a quarter."

Aunt Izzie marched out of the room. When she came back she had something folded up in her hand.

"I didn't know what to give you for Christmas, Katy," she said. "So I thought I'd give you this, and let you choose for yourself. But perhaps you'd rather have it now." So saying, Aunt Izzie laid on the bed a crisp, new five-dollar bill!

"How good you are!" cried Katy.

She gave Aunt Izzie an exact description of the desk she wanted.

"It's no matter about its being very big," said Katy, "but it must have a blue velvet lining, and an inkstand with a silver top.

Oh! And there must be a lock and key. Don't forget that, Aunt Izzie."

"No, I won't. What else?"

"I'd like the sled to be green," continued Katy, "and to have a nice name. If there's enough money left, Aunty, would you buy me a nice book for Dorry and another for Cecy, and a silver thimble for Mary? Oh! And some candy. And something for Debby and Bridget. I think that's all!"

Was ever seven dollars and a quarter expected to do so much? Indeed, Aunt Izzie must have been a witch to make it hold out. But she did, and next day all the precious bundles came home. Everything was exactly right.

"I got 'Snow Skimmer'," said Aunt Izzie.

"It's beautiful," said Katy.

"Oh, hide them, hide them!" she cried with sudden terror. "Somebody's coming." But the somebody was only Papa.

These delightful secrets took up so much of her thoughts that Katy scarcely found time to wonder at the absence of the children, who had hardly been seen for three days. However, after supper they all came up.

"You don't know what we've been doing," began Philly.

"Hush, Phil!" said Clover, in a warning voice. Then she divided the stockings that

166

she held in her hand, and everybody hung them up.

Pretty soon Aunt Izzie came in and swept them all off to bed.

"I know how it will be in the morning," she said, "you'll all be up and racing about as soon as it is light. So you must get your sleep now."

After they had gone, Katy recollected that nobody had offered to hang a stocking up for her. She felt a little hurt when she thought of it.

"But I suppose they forgot," she said to herself quietly.

Katy lay a long time watching the queer shapes of the stockings as they dangled in the firelight. Then she fell asleep.

CHILDREN AND THEIR TOYS

It seemed only a minute before
something touched her and woke her up.
Behold, it was daytime, and there was Philly
in his nightgown, climbing up on the bed to
kiss her! The rest of the children, half
dressed, were dancing about with their
stockings in their hands.

"Merry Christmas! Merry Christmas!"
they cried. "Oh Katy, such beautiful,
beautiful things!"

"Oh!" shrieked Elsie, who at that
moment spied her desk. "Santa Claus did
bring it after all! Why, it's got 'from Katy'
written on it! Oh Katy, it's so sweet and I'm
so happy!" Then Elsie hugged Katy and
sobbed for pleasure.

But what was that strange thing beside

the bed! Katy stared and rubbed her eyes. It certainly had not been there when she went to sleep. How had it got there?

It was a little evergreen tree planted in a red flowerpot. The pot had strips of paper stuck on it, and stars and crosses. The boughs of the tree were hung with oranges and nuts and shiny red apples and popcorn balls and strings of bright berries. There were also a number of little packages tied with blue and crimson ribbon.

"It's a Christmas tree for you, because you're sick, you know!" said the children, all trying to hug her at once.

"We made it ourselves," said Dorry. "I pasted the black stars on the pot."

"And I popped the corn!" cried Philly.

"Do you like it?" asked Elsie, cuddling close to Katy. "That's my present – that one tied with a green ribbon. Don't you want to open them right away?"

Of course Katy wanted to. All sorts of things came out of the little bundles.

Elsie's present was a pen, with a grey kitten on it. Johnnie's, a doll's tea tray of scarlet tin. Dorry's gift, I regret to say, was a huge red-and-yellow spider, which whirred wildly when waved at the end of its string.

"They didn't want me to buy it," he said, "but I did! I thought it would amuse you. Does it amuse you, Katy?"

170

A Family Christmas

"Yes, indeed," said Katy, laughing and blinking as Dorry waved the spider to and fro before her eyes.

"How perfectly lovely everybody is!" said Katy, with grateful tears in her eyes.

That was a pleasant Christmas. The children declared it to be the nicest they had ever had. And though Katy couldn't quite say that, she enjoyed it too, and was very happy.

My Making

An extract from *Memoirs of a London Doll*
by Richard Horne

This tells the story of a Victorian wooden doll.

IN A LARGE, DUSKY ROOM, at the top of a dusky house, there lived a poor doll-maker, whose name was Sprat.

His bench was covered with little wooden legs and arms, wooden heads without hair, small bodies, half legs and half

My Making

arms, which had not yet been fitted
together in the joints, paint pots and
painting brushes, and bits of paper and rags
of all colours.

All the family worked at doll-making.
Mr Sprat was the great manager and doer
of most things, and always the finisher, but
Mrs Sprat painted the eyes, or else fitted in
the glass ones. She also always painted the
eyebrows. The eldest boy painted or glued
hair onto the heads of the best dolls. The
second boy fitted the legs and arms
together. The little girl painted rosy cheeks
and lips, which she always did very nicely,
although sometimes she made them rather
too red.

Now Mr Sprat was very clever. His usual

business was to make jointed dolls
– dolls that could move their legs
and arms in many positions, and
these were made of wood. This
is what I was made out of.

The first thing I remember
was a kind of a pegging and
pushing and scraping and twisting
and tupping down at both sides of me,
above and below.

This was the fitting on of my legs and
arms. Next, my eyes were painted on and I
saw for the first time. Then I was passed
into the hands of the most gentle of all the
Sprat family, and felt something delightfully
warm laid upon my cheeks and mouth. It
was the little girl, who was painting me a

My Making

pair of rosy cheeks and lips, and her face, as she bent over me, was the first thing that my eyes saw. The face was a smiling one, and as I looked up at it I tried to smile too, but I felt some hard material over the outside of my face.

But the last thing done to me was by Mr Sprat himself. He turned me around in his hands, examining and trying my legs and arms, which he moved backwards and forwards, and up and down. I was so frightened! I thought he would break something off me. However, nothing happened, and I was hung upon a line to dry, in the company of many other dolls, both boys and girls.

CHILDREN AND THEIR TOYS

The tops of the beams were also covered with dolls, all waiting there till their paint or varnish had properly dried and hardened.

Mr Sprat was a doll-maker only – he never made doll's clothes. So in about a week, when I was properly dry, Mr Sprat took me down and handed me to his wife. She wrapped me up in silver paper, all but my head, and laying me in a basket among nine others, she carried me off to a large doll shop.

"Place all these dolls on the shelf in the back parlour," said the master of the shop.

As I was carried to the shelf, I caught a glimpse of the shop window. Everything seemed so light! And then, I saw the large crowds of people passing outside in the

My Making

world. Oh, how I longed to be placed in the shop window! I felt I should learn things so fast, if I could only see them.

But I was placed in a dark box, among a number of other dolls, for a long time. And when I was taken out, I was laid upon my back upon a high shelf, with my rosy cheeks and blue eyes turned upwards towards the ceiling.

How long I remained upon the shelf I do not know, but it seemed like years to me.

One day, however, the shop bell rang and a boy came in.

"If you please, sir," said the boy, "do you want a nice cake?"

"Not particularly," answered the master, "but I have no objection to one."

179

"I do not want any money for it, sir," said the boy.

"What do you mean by that?" said the master of the shop.

"Why, sir," said the boy. "I want a nice doll for my sister, and I will give you this cake for a good doll."

"Let me see the cake," said the master. "How did you get it?"

"My grandfather is a baker, sir," answered the boy, "and my sister and I live with him. I went today to deliver seven cakes. But the family at one house had gone away and forgotten the cake, and grandfather told me that my sister and I might have it."

"What is your name?"

My Making

"Thomas Plummy, sir."

"Very well, Thomas Plummy, you may choose any doll you fancy out of that case."

Here some time passed as the boy went from one case to another, always refusing the dolls the master offered him, and when he did choose one himself, the master said it was too expensive.

Presently the master said he had another box full of good dolls in the back room, and in he came. But the boy had followed him to the door, and peeping in, suddenly called out, "There, sir! That one! That is the doll for my cake!" And he pointed his little brown finger up at me.

"Thomas Plummy!" said the master of the shop. "Thomas Plummy! Take the doll and give me that cake. I only hope it may prove good."

"Thank you, sir," said the boy.

At the door he was met by his sister, who had been waiting to receive me in her arms. Then they both ran home, the little girl hugging me close and the boy laughing.

My Making

That evening little Ellen Plummy begged to go to bed earlier than usual. She took me with her, and I had the great happiness of passing the whole night in the arms of my first mamma.

The Dolls and the other Dolls

By Anon

"**M**UMMY," LITTLE NELLIE ASKED, "is it all right to give away things that have been given to you?"

Her mother replied that it might be right sometimes, and she said, "But I should feel a bit sad if I had given a friend a present and she didn't like it, and so was glad to part with it."

"O mother!" said Nellie, "you know how I love my dolls, every one, that my aunts and cousins sent me because I was sick. But now I am well again. There is an appeal for toys to go to the hospital to be presents for sick children. Some sick little girls in the hospital would love a doll. Would it be all right, if I keep only one of my dolls for myself, and send the other five of them for those poor children who haven't any? You don't think my aunts and cousins would mind, do you, if we explained why we were doing it?"

Her mother liked the plan. She gave Nellie a box, labelled for the hospital, and they lined it with some tissue paper, so the dolls wouldn't get bumped on their journey.

Then Nellie began kissing her dolls and laying them, one after another, in the box. First she put in Lady Clarissa, who was very grand. She had long, curling dark hair and a beautiful long, white lace dress. On her feet were the tiniest, daintiest real leather boots that did up with teeny weeny laces.

Then Nellie carefully placed in her little baby doll, who sucked her thumb and looked as if she was asleep. Next, in went

The Dolls and the other Dolls

Alice, a little pocket-sized doll with straight brown hair and a suitcase of tiny clothes to wear. Then she put in Billy, her sailor boy doll with the cheeky smile. And then there were just two left, her favourites. They were nearly the same size, and they looked very alike. Nellie had always called them her twins. The two dolls wore white frocks and blue boots. They had real blonde hair, and their blue eyes would open and shut. These lovely twins Nellie held in her

185

arms a long time before she could decide which one to part with. When she did place one in the box, to be her own no more, a tear was on the doll's cheek (I do not think the drop came from the doll's eye). Her father carried the box down to the hospital, and Nellie watched it go from the window, holding very tight to her last doll.

A few days after the dolls had been given away, Nellie's mother let her invite three little girls to play with her. Each girl brought the doll she had been given for Christmas, and the three dolls, with Nellie's, looked sweet sitting together in a row. The girls chattered and laughed and made the dolls talk and hug each other.

Then Nellie's mother came into her

room, which she had given to the girls to
use that afternoon. She told the children she
would give them a little supper of cakes, ice
cream, pears and grapes, and it would be
ready soon. All the children clapped and
arranged the dolls around a little table, as if
they were going to have food too.

As her mother went out of the room,
Nellie went after her and said softly,
"Mummy, I wouldn't take my dolls back if I
could. I love to think they keep the sick
children amused. But I do wish that for just
a minute we had more dolls at this party."

Her mamma turned to her dressing table.
It stood low enough for the smallest child to
look into the mirror at the back easily.
Moving off the brushes and scent bottles,

she put the four dolls in front of the mirror. Their reflection in the glass showed four more dolls!

"Five, six, seven, eight," cried all of the girls, delighted. "And all are twins – four pairs of twins!"

The Dolls and the other Dolls

And so there were – each doll had her twin in the mirror, just exactly alike. After supper they made the twins sit and stand, and dance, bow and shake hands, in front of the mirror.

So they played till dusk, when the other little girls' mothers came to take them home. After that, whenever Nellie felt lonely for her second twin doll, she would put her doll in front of the mirror, and together they would play with the other little doll that lived inside it.

Bessie's Doll

By Lucy Maud Montgomery

TOMMY PUFFER stopped to look at Miss Octavia's flowers. Miss Octavia always had the prettiest garden in Arundel. He was still looking when Miss Octavia herself came out of the house.

"Here, you, get away!" she said sharply.

Bessie's Doll

"I was just looking at the flowers,"
Tommy replied.

"Yes, and picking out the next one to
throw a stone at," said Miss Octavia
sarcastically. "It was you who broke my big
geranium the other day."

"It wasn't," said Tommy.

"You clear out of here or I'll make you,"
she said warningly.

So Tommy raged along the street until
he came to Mr Blacklock's store. In the
window he saw something that put
Miss Octavia's remarks out of his head.

This was a doll. It was beautifully dressed
in blue silk, with a ruffled blue silk hat. The
doll had lovely long golden hair, big brown
eyes and pink cheeks, and it stood right up

191

in the showcase and held out its hands.

"Gee, ain't it a beauty!" said Tommy admiringly. "I must go and bring Bessie to see it."

Bessie was eight years old and walked with a crutch. The very first time she had seen Tommy she had smiled at him and said, "Good morning." From that moment Tommy was her friend.

Tommy found Bessie sitting by the kitchen window.

"Bessie, come for a walk up to Mr Blacklock's store," he said eagerly. "There is something I want to show you."

Bessie reached for her crutch and the two of them went up to the store. Just before they reached it, Tommy made Bessie shut her eyes and led her to the window.

"Now – look!" Tommy commanded dramatically.

"Oh, Tommy, isn't she perfectly beautiful?" Bessie said. "Oh, she's the very loveliest dolly I ever saw."

"I thought you'd like her," said Tommy. "Don't you wish you had a doll like that of your very own, Bessie?"

"Of course I could never have a dolly like that," she said. "She must cost an awful lot. Tommy, will you bring me up here every day to look at her?"

193

"Of course," said Tommy.

Bessie talked about the doll all the way home. "I'm going to call her Roselle Geraldine," she said. After that she went up to see Roselle Geraldine every day, gazing at her for long moments.

Sometimes, though, Tommy felt uneasy. What would Bessie do when the doll was sold, as would probably happen soon? Tommy thought Bessie would feel awfully sad, and he would be responsible for it.

What Tommy feared came to pass. One afternoon the doll was not in the window.

"Oh," cried Bessie, bursting into tears. "She's gone – Roselle Geraldine is gone."

"Perhaps she isn't sold," said Tommy comfortingly. "I'll go in and ask."

Bessie's Doll

A minute later Tommy came out.

"Yes, she's sold," he said. "Mr Blacklock sold her to a lady yesterday. Don't cry, Bessie – maybe they'll put another in the window before long."

"It won't be mine," sobbed Bessie. "It won't be Roselle Geraldine."

Bessie cried quietly all the way home, and Tommy could not comfort her. He wished he had never shown her the doll in the window.

"If only I was rich," said Tommy to himself miserably. "I'd buy her a cartload of dolls. But I can't do nothing."

By this time Tommy had reached the fence in front of Miss Octavia's lawn, and he stopped to look over it. But there was not much to see this time – only the well-weeded beds, and the long curves of dahlia plants, which Miss Octavia had set out a few days before. Tommy knew Miss Octavia was away. He had heard her telling her friend that she would not be back until the next day.

Tommy was still leaning moodily against the fence when Mrs Jenkins and Mrs Reid came by, and they also paused to look at the garden.

"Dear me, how cold it is!" shivered Mrs Reid. "There's going to be a hard frost tonight. Miss Octavia's flowers will be nipped as sure as anything."

"Her brother's wife is sick," said Mrs Jenkins. "She'll feel awfully bad if her flowers get frosted, especially those dahlias."

Mrs Jenkins and Mrs Reid moved away, leaving Tommy by the fence. It was cold – there was going to be a hard frost – and Miss Octavia's plants and flowers would certainly be spoiled. Tommy thought he ought to be glad, but he wasn't. He was sorry – not for Miss Octavia, but for her flowers. He wished he could save them.

And couldn't he? Tommy knew that newspapers spread over the beds and tied around the dahlias would save them. He had seen Miss Octavia doing it in other springs. And he knew there was a big box of newspapers in a little shed in her backyard.

Tommy hurried home quickly and got a ball of twine out of his few treasures. Then

199

he went back to Miss Octavia's garden.

The next morning Miss Octavia got off the train with a grim face. There had been a bad frost. All along the road Miss Octavia had seen gardens spoiled. She knew what she should see when she got to her own garden – the dahlia stalks drooping and black and limp.

But she didn't. Instead she saw every dahlia carefully tied up in a newspaper, and newspapers spread out over all the beds, held neatly in place with pebbles. Nothing was spoiled – everything was safe.

Who could have done it? Miss Octavia was puzzled. On one side of her lived Miss Matheson, who spent all her time on the sofa. So to Miss Matheson's house Miss Octavia went.

"Rachel, do you know who covered my plants up last night?"

Miss Matheson nodded. "Yes, it was Tommy Puffer. I saw him working away."

Miss Octavia went back to her house

feeling rather ashamed of herself when she remembered how she had always treated Tommy Puffer.

"There must be some good in the child, or he wouldn't have done this," she said to herself. "I've been real mean, but I'll make it up to him."

When Tommy passed her house the next morning, Miss Octavia ran to the door and called him.

"Tommy, Miss Matheson tells me that it was you who saved my flowers from the frost the other night. I'm very grateful to you indeed. Whatever made you think of doing it?"

"I hated to see the flowers spoiled," muttered Tommy.

200

Bessie's Doll

"Well, it was real thoughtful of you. I'm sorry I've been so hard on you, Tommy. Is there anything I can do for you — anything you'd like to have? If it's in reason I'll get it for you, just to pay my debt."

Tommy stared at Miss Octavia with a sudden hope. "Oh, Miss Octavia," he cried eagerly, "would you buy a doll and give it to me?"

"A doll! What on earth do you want with a doll?"

"It's for Bessie," said Tommy eagerly. Then he told Miss Octavia the whole story. Miss Octavia listened silently, sometimes nodding her head. When he had finished she walked away, but soon returned, bringing with her the very doll that had been in Mr Blacklock's window.

"I guess this is the doll," she said. "I bought it to give to a small niece of mine, but I can get another for her. You may take this to Bessie."

It would be of no use to try to describe Bessie's joy when Tommy rushed in and put Roselle Geraldine in her arms. From that moment Bessie was the happiest little lassie in Arundel.

202

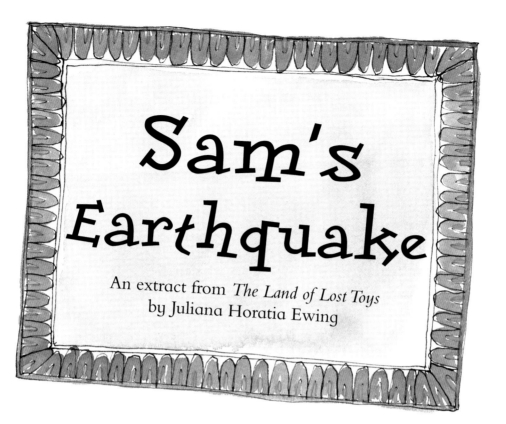

Sam's Earthquake

An extract from *The Land of Lost Toys*
by Juliana Horatia Ewing

SAM HAD ALWAYS had the knack of
breaking his own toys. He also
sometimes broke other people's, and his twin
sister Dot was long-suffering.

Dot was firm, quick-witted and unselfish.
When Sam scalped her new doll, and tied

the black curls to a wigwam made from the curtains of a four-poster bed, Dot was upset. When she saw the hairless doll on the floor, she burst into tears. But in a moment she clenched her fists, forced back the tears and cried out, "I don't care."

Sam was sorry, and Dot was heroic and never told on him. There are, however, limits to everything. An earthquake celebrated with the whole contents of the toy cupboard was more than even she could bear.

It happened like this. Early one morning, Sam announced that he was going to give a grand show. He refused to share his plans with Dot, but he begged her to lend him all the toys she had, in return for which she was to be the only audience.

Sam's Earthquake

Dot tried hard to learn the secret, and to keep back some of her things. But Sam would tell her nothing, and he wanted all of her toys.

Dot gave them, and watched Sam carrying pieces of board and a green table cover into the nursery. At last, Sam threw open the door and ushered her into the rocking chair.

On a sort of table covered with green cloth, Sam had arranged all the toys to look roughly like a town, with its streets and buildings. It was not Sam's fault that

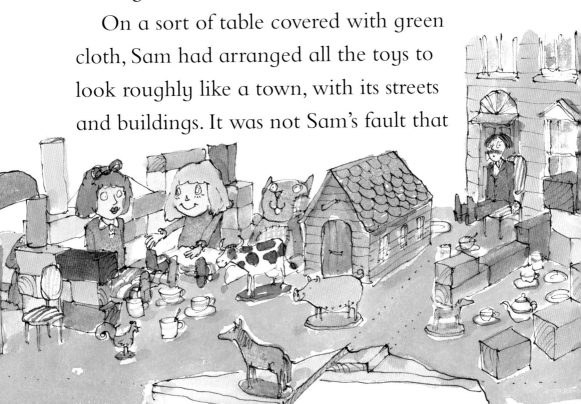

the doll's house, the farm, his own brick buildings and the cottages were all totally different sizes. The big dolls were seated in a building, made with the wooden bricks, and were taking tea out of Dot's new, china, doll's tea set.

Dot clapped loudly.

"Here, ladies and gentlemen," said Sam, "you see the great city of Lisbon, the capital of Portugal—"

Dot cheered and rocked herself to and fro in enjoyment.

"In this house," Sam said, "a party of Portuguese ladies are taking tea together."

"Breakfast, you mean," said Dot. "You said it was in the morning, you know."

"Well, they took tea for their breakfast,"

said Sam. "Don't interrupt me, Dot. You are the audience and you mustn't speak. Here you see two peasants – no! They are not Noah and his wife, Dot, and if you go on talking I shall shut up. I say they are peasants, peacefully driving cattle. At this moment a rumbling sound startles everyone in the city." Here Sam rolled some croquet balls around in a box, but the dolls sat as quiet as before, and only Dot was startled.

"This was succeeded by a slight shock." Here Sam shook the table, which upset some of the buildings.

"Some houses fell," Sam continued.

Dot began to look anxious.

"This shock was followed by others—"

"Take care," Dot begged.

CHILDREN AND THEIR TOYS

"—of greater strength."

"Oh, Sam!" Dot shrieked, jumping up.
"You're breaking the china!"

"The largest buildings shook," Sam said.

"Sam! Sam! The doll's house is falling,"
Dot cried, making wild efforts to save it.
But Sam held her back with one arm,

while with the other he began to pull at the boards that formed his table.

"Suddenly the ground split and opened with a fearful yawn." Sam jerked out the boards, and the doll's house, brick buildings, the farm and all the toys sank together in ruins.

"And in a moment the whole city of Lisbon was swallowed up," Sam continued. "Dot! Dot! What's the matter? It's splendid fun. Things must be broken sometimes, and I'm sure it was exactly like the real thing. Dot! You don't care, do you? I didn't think you'd mind it. It was such a splendid earthquake."

But Dot was gasping and choking, and when at last she found breath, it was only to throw herself on her face upon the floor in tears. And Sam was sent to bed for the rest of the day. It was not until the next day that he came down.

"Oh, Dot!" Sam said, as soon as he could get her into a corner. "I am so very, very sorry! Particularly about the tea things."

"Never mind," said Dot, "I don't care."

"I have an idea to make up – will you help me, Dot?" cried Sam.

"What do you want?" asked Dot.

210

"It's the glue pot," Sam continued. "It does take so long to boil. And I have been stirring at the glue with a stick forever so long to get it to melt. It is very hot work. I wish you would take it for a bit. It's as much for your good as for mine."

"Is it?" said Dot. "What is the idea?"

"I won't tell you until I have finished my shop. I want to get to it now, and I wish you would take a turn at the glue pot."

By this time Sam had set up business in the window seat, and was fastening a large paper notice over his shop. It said:

MR SAM
Dolls Doctor and Toymender

211

"Splendid!" shouted Dot.

Sam took the glue pot and began to bustle about.

"Now, Dot, get me all the broken toys, and we'll see what we can do. And here's a second idea. Do you see that box? Into that we shall put all the toys that are quite spoiled and cannot possibly be mended. For the future when I want a doll to spoil, I shall go to that box, and the same with any other toy that I want to destroy. I shall mend the dolls free, and keep all the furniture in repair."

Sam really kept his word. He had a natural turn for skilful mending, and looked after many a broken doll and chipped cup. When his birthday came round, which was

212

some months after these events, Dot (helped by her mother and Aunt Penelope) had prepared a surprise for him that was at least as good as any of his own 'splendid ideas'.

All the toys were assembled on the table to give Sam their present – a fine box of carpenter's tools as a reward for his services.

And certain gaps in the china tea set, some scars on the dolls' faces, and a good many new legs, both among the furniture and the animals, are now the only remaining traces of Sam's earthquake.

Adventures and Troubles

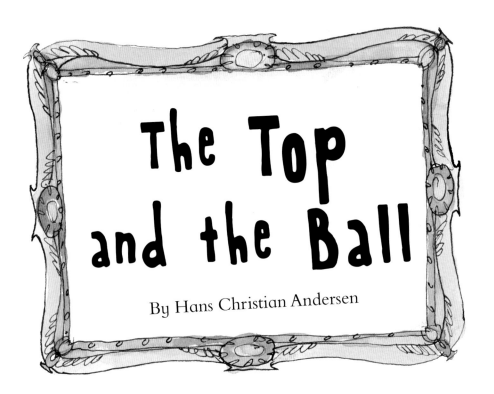

The Top and the Ball

By Hans Christian Andersen

This story was written before balls were made of rubber, so to help a ball bounce it was filled with cork, which is quite bouncy.

A **TOP AND A BALL** lay together in a box, among other toys, and the top said to the ball, "Shall we be married, as we live in the same box?"

But the ball, which wore a dress of

The Top and the Ball

leather and thought a lot of herself, would not even reply.

The next day, the little boy to whom the playthings belonged came along. He painted the top red and yellow, and banged a brass-headed nail into the middle, so that while the top was spinning round it looked quite splendid.

"Look at me," said the top to the ball. "What do you say now? Shall we be engaged to each other? We would suit so well – you bounce and I dance. No one could be happier than we would be."

"Do you think so? Perhaps you do not know that my father and mother were leather slippers, and that I have a Spanish cork in my body," replied the ball.

"Yes, but I am made of mahogany," said the top.

"You certainly know how to speak for yourself very well," said the ball, "but I cannot marry you. I am almost engaged to a swallow. Every time I bounce up in the air, he puts his head out of the nest and says, 'Will you?' and I have said, 'Yes' to myself silently, and that is as good as being half engaged, but I will promise never to forget you."

"Much good that will be to me," said the top, and they spoke to each other no more.

Next day the ball was taken out by the boy. The top saw it bouncing high in the air, like a bird, till it went nearly out of sight. Each time it came back, and as it touched the earth, it gave a higher leap than before, either because it longed to fly upwards, or from having a Spanish cork in its body. But the ninth time it rose in the air, it remained away and did not return. The boy searched everywhere for the ball, but it was in vain, for it could not be found – the ball was gone.

"I know very well where she is," sighed the top, "she is in the swallow's nest, and has married the swallow."

The more the top thought of this, the more he longed for the ball. His love increased the more, just because he could not get her, and that she should have been won by another was the worst of all. The top still twirled about and hummed, but he continued to think of the ball, and the more he thought of her, the more beautiful she seemed to him.

Several years passed by, and the top was no longer young, but there came a day when he looked handsomer than ever, for the boy painted him gold all over. He whirled and danced about till he hummed quite loud, and was something worth looking at. But one day he leapt too high, and then he, also, was gone. They searched everywhere, even in the cellar, but he was nowhere to be found. Where could he be? He had fallen into the dust bin, where all sorts of rubbish was lying – cabbage stalks, dust and rain droppings that had fallen down from the gutter under the roof.

"Now I am in a fix," he said, "my gold paint will soon be washed off here. Oh dear, what a set of rubbish I have got among!" And then he glanced at a curious round thing, like an old apple, which lay near a long, leafless cabbage stalk. It was, however, not an apple, but an old ball, which had lain for years in the gutter and was soaked through with water.

"Thank goodness, here comes someone I can talk to," said the ball, looking at the

gold top. "I am made of leather," she said.
"I was sewn together by a young lady, and
I have a Spanish cork in my body. But no
one would think it, to look at me now. I was
once engaged to a swallow, but I fell in here
from the gutter. I have lain here more than
five years and have been thoroughly

soaked. Believe me, it is a long time."

The top said nothing. He thought of his old love, and the more she said, the more clear it became to him that this was the same ball.

A woman then came to clean out the dust bin. "Ah," she exclaimed, "here is the gold top."

So the top was brought back into the house where everyone was proud of it, but nothing more was heard of the ball. The top spoke not a word about his old love, for that had soon died away.

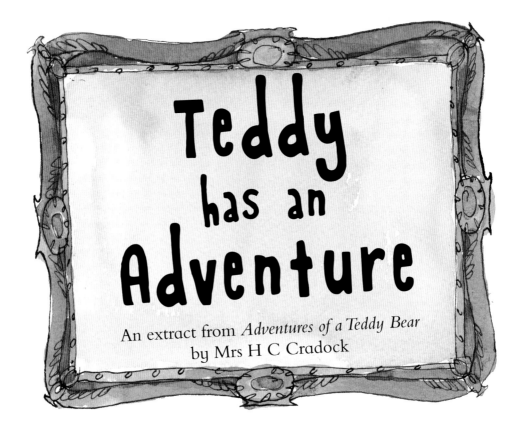

Teddy has an Adventure

An extract from *Adventures of a Teddy Bear*
by Mrs H C Cradock

*Teddy lives with his owner, a little girl he calls Mummy, and
his friends, Owly, a stuffed owl, and John, a toy elephant.*

TEDDY SAT ON HIS LOW CHAIR,
thinking. "It is time," he said, "that I
had an adventure." He had heard people
talking about adventures, but he wasn't
quite sure what they were. "At any rate," he

Teddy has an Adventure

said, "I must set off and go away somewhere. I don't think I can have an adventure sitting here."

For a minute he sat very still – he was evidently thinking hard.

"I shall have to take a little luggage with me – just a few things I must have. I'll write a list like Mummy does."

When they had all been to the sea last year, Mummy had written down things she did not want to forget to take with her, like her spade, bucket, ball and picture book.

So Teddy felt in his pocket for his little notebook, a blue one, and began to write.

"Hanky," he said to himself, writing it down, "biscuits, honey, a little string, a knife – in case."

He said "in case" meaning that something might turn up suddenly that perhaps he would want to cut. "You never know," he said. Then he sat quiet again.

'Perhaps a little money too,' he thought, 'in case.'

Teddy went to the cupboard and got out his purse, a man's proper leather purse. Looking into it to see how much money he had, he found three pennies. Some people would have called them Tiddlywink counters – but he called them pennies. One was blue, one red and one green. The blue one was larger than the others, so he

226

Teddy has an Adventure

thought he could buy more with that.

'Oh, a walking-stick,' he thought. 'That I must have.' So he wrote 'Walking-stick' in his notebook.

For just a moment he wondered if he should tell the others – John and Owly.

"No," he decided. They would certainly want to come too, and this time he wanted to go off by himself. He was really a very good-tempered little bear and not at all selfish, but he said, "Sometimes a bear wants to be alone."

So he just said to Mummy, when Owly was asleep and John was too busy with his own affairs to pay attention to Teddy, "I'm going away – for a walk."

"Are you, Teddy?" said Mummy. "That

will be very nice! All by yourself?"

"Yes," he said. He was really feeling excited, for he had never done such a thing before. But he didn't want Mummy to know that his heart was beating fast and that his breathing felt rather funny.

"Yes," he said again, trying to speak calmly. He put on an important sort of grown-up look, which meant, "I'm busy now, so I can't talk anymore." He was dreadfully afraid of letting out his secret.

"When are you coming back?" Mummy asked him.

"I'm not quite sure," he said. "Perhaps I'll write and tell you."

"But you'll be back before bedtime, I suppose?" Mummy said.

Teddy has an Adventure

"I'll see," said Teddy, "Perhaps I'll write," he said again. He rather liked the idea of sending Mummy a letter.

Teddy was feeling very excited now. Then when nobody was noticing he started off. He had his small rucksack strapped over his shoulder and his walking-stick in his hand.

At last he was off. He walked along a country lane, holding his head up and taking long strides. Every now and then he looked at his watch.

"Ten o'clock," he said. "I wonder what John and Owly are doing now? I suspect they are saying, 'I wish Teddy was here. I wonder where he is?' Perhaps they are looking about everywhere for me. They know little of where I am."

Now Teddy's legs were not very long, and soon his strides became shorter, then shorter still, and at last he decided that a rest would be a good thing.

"What about a little lunch?" he said to himself. He found a mossy bank and was very glad to sit down.

"A little honey now," he said. "I think that would be a very good idea. And a biscuit dipped into it. What a good thing I brought my hanky! – for stickiness! You never know. Mummy sometimes says, 'Always take a hanky everywhere. That is the safe thing to do.'"

Then he twisted his rucksack round from his back, and was just beginning to open it

Teddy has an Adventure

when he felt something oozing through the bottom of it.

Alas! It was the honey. He had put it into a little jar with a cork to keep it safe, but the cork had come out.

"Oh, dear!" Teddy said. However, as there was no one near to say anything about his manners, he went on, "I will lick some of the honey up. I dare say it will taste quite nice, and it is a pity to waste it. Waste not, want not."

He didn't quite know what these last words meant, but he thought they must mean something.

"Yes, waste not, want not," he said again, giving his rucksack a lick.

He found a bit of broken biscuit at the

bottom of his rucksack, rubbed it on the stickiness and ate it!

He kept saying, "Waste not, want not. I was hungry."

But Teddy didn't feel happy about his stickiness, for he was a very well brought-up little bear.

"Something must be done about this," he said. He looked round, and to his great joy he found a small stream below and behind the bank on which he was sitting.

"The very thing!" he said.

He set to work to make himself clean, and a great business it was. He was sticky almost all over. "My hanky has come in useful," he said.

"This is the first of my adventures –

getting sticky, and finding a stream close by.
Now I think a little sleep wouldn't be a bad
idea. I wonder what John and Owly are
doing? I suspect—"

But he dropped off to sleep before he had
begun to wonder.

Playing with Fire

An extract from *Memoirs of a London Doll*
by Richard Horne

*The London doll is now owned by Lady Flora, the daughter
of a countess. There is going to be a ball, and her mother has
ordered matching dresses for her and her doll.*

AT LAST THE DRESSES came home.
They were beautiful and both exactly
alike. They were made of the thinnest white
gauze, to be worn over very full petticoats
of the same white gauze, so that they stuck

out very much. They were trimmed with an imitation of lily of the valley, made in white satin and silver. The trousers were of white satin, trimmed with gauze.

The day of the ball was rather cold and windy, so a fire was ordered in Lady Flora's bedroom. Towards evening the dresses were all laid out ready to put on, but when my mamma saw them she could not wait, and insisted upon being dressed. Still there was a long time to wait, so Lady Flora took me in her arms and began to dance.

Playing with Fire

In doing this she noticed that each time she turned, her full frock gave the fire a puff, so that a blaze came. As she was amused by it, she whisked round quicker in order to make the blaze greater.

"Oh, Lady Flora!" cried her maid. "Take care of your dress! Wait till I run and fetch the fireguards."

Away ran the maid to fetch the fireguards, and while she was gone Lady Flora decided to dance for the last time. The next time she did it she went just the least bit too near, and her frock was in a blaze in a moment!

She gave a loud scream and a jump, and was going to run, when most fortunately her foot caught one corner of a thick rug, and down she fell. This smothered the blaze, but still her clothes were on fire, and she lay shrieking and rolling on the floor.

Up ran the countess and rolled the thick rug all around her, and carried her in her arms to her own room.

Physicians were sent for, and all the burnt things were taken off and thrown on one side. I lay among these. My beautiful dress was all black, but I was not really much burned, nor was Lady Flora. A few weeks might cure her but what could cure me? I was so scorched and frizzled that the paint that was on my skin had blistered and peeled off. I was quite black. No notice was taken of me, and I was thrown by one of the servants out of a back window.

A fine large dog,
who was just passing,
thought somebody had thrown him a bone.
So he caught me up in his mouth and away
he ran with me, wagging his tail.

Turning down first one street, then
another, he soon stopped at a door, upon
which was written:

J. C. Johnson, Portrait Painter

The dog ran up the stairs (three flights) until he came to the front room of the second floor, and in he bounced. There sat a little girl and her aunt, and Mr J. C. Johnson was painting the aunt's portrait.

The dog ran at once to the little girl and, laying me at her feet, then sprang back a step or two. He began wagging and swishing his tail about, waiting to be praised and patted and called a good dog.

"Oh, Nep!" cried the aunt to the dog, "what horrid thing have you brought?"

"It is an Indian statue, I believe," said Mr Johnson, "an Indian statue of ebony, much worn by time."

"I think," said the little girl, to whom Mr Johnson handed me, "I think it looks very like a wooden doll, with a burnt frock and scorched face."

"Well, so it is, I do believe," said the aunt.

"Let me look once more," said the portrait painter. "Yes, yes, madam, your niece is correct. It is not a work of Indian art, it is the work of a London doll-maker."

"Oh, you poor London doll!" said the little girl. "What a pity you were not made in India, or somewhere a wonderful way off, then Mr Johnson would have taken pity on you, and painted you all over."

Mr Johnson laughed at this, and then gave a good-natured look at me. "Well, my dear, leave this little doll with me, and when you come again with your aunt, you shall see what I have done."

241

The aunt thanked Mr Johnson for his promise, and away they went, the Newfoundland dog, Nep, leaping downstairs before them, to show the way.

As soon as they were gone, Mr Johnson told his son to tear off all my burnt clothes, scrape me all over with the back of a knife, and then wash me well with soap and water. When I was dry, he painted me all over with a warm colour, like flesh, and when that was dry, he painted my cheeks, lips and

242

Playing with Fire

eyebrows, and finally he gave me a
complete skin of the most delicate varnish.

My beautiful hair was entirely burned
off. So the kind Mr Johnson took the
measure of my head, and went to a shop
and bought me a most lovely, dark, auburn
wig, with long ringlets, and his son glued it
on. When all was done, they hung me up
in a safe place to dry.

When the little girl and her
aunt came again to the portrait
painter's house, he presented me
to her with a smiling face. "There,
Miss Mary," he said, "you see I have been
at work upon this doll of yours."

Mary gave Mr Johnson many, many
thanks for his kindness in taking so much

pain about me. Then she went downstairs, tossing me up in the air for joy and catching me as I was falling. This frightened me very much and I was so glad when we got downstairs.

And so I found a new mamma.

Adventure in the Attic

By Mrs Molesworth

This is a mother telling her children about an adventure she had when she was little. She lived in Queen Victoria's time, when people travelled with trunks instead of suitcases. A trunk was a big, heavy box, usually made of leather and wood. The mother's big sister, Helen, looked after her. The little girl, May, also calls her Nelly.

ONE DAY, Helen told me that Grandfather was going to take her and me to spend Christmas with one of our aunts in London. I was always talking and thinking about how nice it would be, and wanting to know what trunks we should take, and if all my dolls might go.

I got in the way of going up to the big attic where the trunks were kept, and of looking at them. There was one trunk in particular that took my fancy. It was old-fashioned and inside it had several divisions, some with little lids of their own, and I used to think how nice it would be for me. I could put all my dolls in so beautifully, and each would have a kind of house for itself.

At last, one day I said to my sister, "Helen, may I have the big trunk with the little cupboards in it for my trunk?"

Helen was busy at the time, and I don't think she heard exactly what I said.

Adventure in the Attic

"May I begin putting Marietta and Lady Regina into the little cupboards inside?" I asked.

"Oh yes, I daresay you can if you like," said Helen. She told me afterwards that when I spoke of cupboards she never thought I meant a trunk.

I fell asleep with my head full of how nicely I could put the dolls into the trunk, each with her clothes beside her.

The very first thing the next morning, I got them all together and I climbed up to the attic with my dolls, Lady Regina under one arm and Marietta under the other, and a bundle of their clothes. The trunk was open and I managed to lift out the two top trays. One of them was much larger than the other, and it was in what I called the cupboards. There were two of these and each had a lid.

I went on for a little time, laying in some of the clothes first to make a nice soft place for the dolls to lie on, but I soon got tired. It was so very far to reach over. It came into my head that it would be much easier to get into the box myself – I could stand in the big hole and reach over to the little divisions, where I wanted to put the dolls, and it would be far less tiring than trying to reach from the outside.

So I clambered in – it was not very difficult – and when I found myself really inside the trunk, I was so pleased that I sat down cross-legged.

I soon jumped up again, meaning to
reach over for Lady Regina, but, how it
happened I cannot tell, I suppose I
somehow caught the tapes that fastened the

lid, any way down it came. Before I knew
what had happened, I found myself doubled
up somehow, with the heavy lid on top of
me, all in the dark, except for a little line of
light around the edge. For the lid had not
shut quite down – the hasp of the lock (as
the little sticking-out piece is called) had
caught in the fall, and was wedged into a
wrong place. So, luckily for me, there was
still a space for some air to come in and a
little light, though very little.

I was dreadfully frightened at first, then I
began to get over my fright, and to struggle
to get out. I kicked and I pushed but it was
no use – the strong heavy lid would not
move. I tried to poke out my fingers
through the little space that was left, but I

could not find the lock. At last I thought of another plan. I set to work screaming.

I kicked and screamed, and at last I burst into tears and roared. Then I caught sight, through the chink, of Lady Regina's blue dress, where the doll was lying on the floor near the trunk.

"Nasty Regina," I shouted. "You are lying there as if there was nothing the matter, and it was all for you I came up here. I hate dolls – they never do anything. If you were a little dog you would go and bark, and then somebody would come and let me out."

Then I went on crying and sobbing until I was perfectly tired, and then what do you think I did? Although I was uncomfortable,

all crushed up into a little ball, I went to
sleep! I went to sleep as soundly as if I had
been in my own little bed. When I woke up
I could not think where I was. All of a
sudden I thought I heard a sound –
someone was coming upstairs and then I
heard voices.

"Fallen out of the window," one said.
"Oh no nurse, she couldn't!"

And then I called out, "Oh Nelly, Nelly!
I'm here! I'm shut up in the big box with
the cupboards!"

She heard me. Dear Nelly! I never have
called to her in vain, children, in all my life.
And in half a minute she had dashed up the
stairs and, guided by my voice, was kneeling
down beside the trunk.

"Little May, my poor little May," Nelly called out, and do you know I really think she was crying too!

I was – by the time Nelly had got the lid unhooked and raised, and had lifted me out – in floods of tears. I clung to Nelly and told her how dreadful it had been, and she petted me so that I am afraid I quite forgot it was all my own fault.

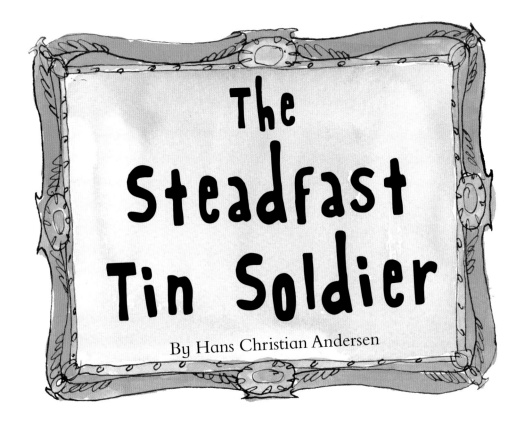

The Steadfast Tin Soldier

By Hans Christian Andersen

THERE WERE ONCE UPON A TIME twenty-five tin soldiers. They wore smart uniforms, and proudly shouldered their guns and looked straight ahead.

The first words that they heard in this world, when the lid of their box was taken off, were, "Hooray, tin soldiers!" This was

254

The Steadfast Tin Soldier

shouted by a little boy. They had been given to him because it was his birthday, and now he began setting them out on the table.

Each soldier was exactly like the other, except just one, who had been made last when the tin had run short. But he stood as firmly on his one leg as the others did on two, and he is the one that became famous.

There were many other toys on the table on which the tin soldiers were being set out, but the nicest of all was a little castle. In front of the castle stood some trees surrounding a tiny mirror, which looked like a lake.

That was all very pretty, but the most beautiful thing was a little lady, who stood in the open doorway. She was cut out of paper, but she had on a dress of the finest muslin, with a scarf of narrow blue ribbon around her shoulders.

The beautiful little lady was stretching out both her arms, for she was a dancer. She was lifting up one of her legs so high in the air that the tin soldier couldn't see it anywhere, and thought that she, too, had only one leg.

'That's the wife for me!' he thought, 'but she is so grand and lives in a castle, while I have only a box. But still, I must get to know her.'

When the night came, all of the toys began to play, dancing and fighting. Some of the tin soldiers rattled in their box, for they wanted to be out too, but could not raise the lid. The dolls played at leap-frog and all of the pencils ran about!

The only two who did not stir from their places were the tin soldier and the little dancer. She remained on tip-toe, with both arms outstretched, and the soldier stood steadfastly on his one leg, never moving his

257

eyes from her face.

When it was morning, and the children had got up, the tin soldier was put in the windowsill. All at once, the window flew open and out fell the little tin soldier, head over heels, from the third-storey window! That was a terrible fall, I can tell you! The tin soldier landed on his head with his leg in the air, his gun being wedged between two paving-stones.

The little boy came down at once to look for him, but, although he was so near him that he almost trod on him, he did not notice him.

Soon it began to drizzle. Then the drops of rain came down faster and there was a regular downpour. When it was over, two little boys came along.

"Just look!" cried one. "Here is a tin soldier! We shall make him sail up and down in a boat!"

So they made a little boat out of newspaper, put the tin soldier in it, and made him sail up and down the gutter.

The paper-boat tossed up and down. In the middle of the stream it went so quickly that the tin soldier trembled, but he remained steadfast, looking straight ahead of him.

All at once the boat passed under a long tunnel that was as dark as the tin soldier's box had been.

'Where can I be going now?' he thought. 'Oh dear!'

259

Suddenly there came along a great water-rat that lived in the tunnel.

"Have you got a passport?" asked the rat. "Out with your passport!"

But the tin soldier was silent and grasped his gun more firmly.

The boat sped on and left the water-rat behind it. But the current became swifter and stronger. The tin soldier could see daylight, but in his ears there sounded a roaring enough to frighten any brave man. At the end of the tunnel the gutter emptied into a great canal – that would be just as dangerous for the tin soldier as it would be for us to go down a waterfall!

On went the boat, the poor tin soldier keeping himself as stiff as he could – no one

should say of him that he had trembled. The boat whirled three, four times around, and became filled to the brim with water! The tin soldier was standing up to his neck in water, and deeper and deeper sank the boat, and softer and softer grew the paper.

The paper came in two and the tin soldier fell – but at that moment he was swallowed by a great fish.

How dark it was inside, even darker than in the tunnel! But there the steadfast tin soldier lay full length, shouldering his gun.

Up and down swam the fish, then it became quite still. Suddenly it was as if a flash of lightning had passed through it, the daylight streamed in, and a voice exclaimed, "Why, here is the tin soldier!"

The Steadfast Tin Soldier

The fish had been caught, taken to market, sold, and brought into the kitchen, where the cook had cut it open. She took up the tin soldier and carried him into a room, where everyone wanted to see the hero who had been found inside a fish. But the tin soldier was not at all proud.

They put him on the table and the tin soldier was in the same room in which he had been before! He saw the same children and the same toys, and there was the same grand castle with the pretty little dancer. She was still standing on one leg with the other high in the air – she too was steadfast.

Trouble with Tar Marbles

By Anon

A very popular game for boys used to be playing with marbles. Boys would have competitions to try and win each other's marbles. Coal tar was used to make road surfaces shiny.

MY FONDNESS FOR MARBLES began very early, and when I was about seven years old led me into an adventure. I already had a large number of marbles, when one day I overheard my eldest

brother telling one of his schoolmates that
he had discovered that marbles could be
made from coal tar, of which there
was a large heap on a street in
a distant part of the town. He
showed the marbles he had
made – black, round
and glossy.

My brother told
me where the heap was
to be found and, in the
afternoon, I started off to find the
spot and collect a supply of coal tar, which
I could make into marbles at home.
Delightful visions of bags filled with
marbles danced through my brain.

It was a very hot July afternoon, and I

was well warmed up and puffing by the time I got there. But the sight of the heaps of coal tar put all thoughts quite out of my head – it also caused me to forget that I had on new clothes.

I don't need to tell you that I didn't know much about coal tar. The only thing I knew about it was that it could be moulded into any shape I pleased. I had no idea that it is just like ordinary tar, in that it melts with heat and becomes the toughest, stickiest, most unmanageable thing with which a small boy can come into contact.

I fell to work to collect what I wanted to carry home. I filled the pockets of my trousers and of my jacket, and lastly, when these were stuffed, I filled the crown of my hat so full that it would hardly go on my head. The place was at some distance from my home, and I did not want to have to come back for more.

I started off towards home. It had been a long walk, and I was pretty tired, but I was also in a great hurry to begin making marbles, so I walked as fast as I could. After a little time I began to have a nasty feeling of stickiness about my waist, and a trickling sensation in the region of my knees.

A thought flitted across my mind – perhaps coal tar might melt?

A very slight inspection of my pockets proved to me that coal tar can melt and become liquid, and the black streams that began to trickle down the sides of my face were a second proof. I tried to take off my hat, but it would not come. I tried to get the tar out of my pockets, but only succeeded in getting my hands covered with the black, horrible stuff.

I seated myself on the ground and tried to scrape off the black spots, while I could feel small streams coming down inside of the collar of my shirt. I got a good deal of the coal tar off, but there seemed to be even more of it on. Then I gave up in despair and burst into tears.

I set off home with a nervous mind. My

clothes were ruined and I was covered in stickiness from head to toe. I dreaded what my parents would say when they saw me.

When I reached home I thought I would avoid all trouble, for that night at least, by going quietly up the back stairs, going to bed and playing sick.

I reached the bedroom without being seen and, just as I was, with my hat on, I got into bed and covered myself entirely up with the bedclothes. It was now dusk and I felt for the moment quite safe.

Presently my aunt came into the room to get something for which she was looking. I could hear her give several inquiring sniffs, and as she went out I heard her say, "I certainly do smell tar – where can it possibly be coming from?"

Then in came my mother. "Tar? Smell tar?" she said. "Of course you do, it's strong enough in this room. Bring a light."

It was the sound of doom!

My mother soon came close up to the bed. She held the light so that it fell full upon me as she tried to turn down the bedclothes. Her exclamations and shrieks of laughter brought every member of the household to the room, and as one after another came in, each one burst into howls of laughter.

I had now become stuck in the bedclothes like a caterpillar in its chrysalis, and I knew that if I sat up, with the pillow stuck fast to my hat, the sight of me would only bring more laughter.

I declared if they would all go away except my mother, I would tell her all about

it. The crowd left, under orders to send up a bottle of oil, a tub of hot water and a pair of shears.

After my clothes had been cut to

ribbons, the sheets torn up, my head practically shaved, and my body washed first in oil and then hot soapsuds, I finally came clean, though I still had a grey look for several days.

And I never did make any marbles of coal tar!

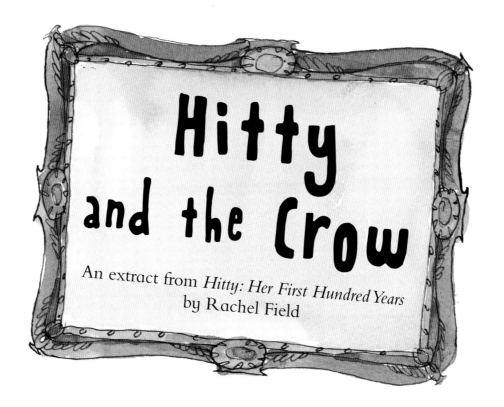

Hitty and the Crow

An extract from *Hitty: Her First Hundred Years* by Rachel Field

Hitty is a small wooden doll, much loved by her owner Phoebe. She has been left out in the grass one day.

IT HAPPENED SO QUICKLY that I have no very clear idea of how it actually came about. I had heard distant cawing all that afternoon and I had been vaguely aware that crows were in the nearby trees. But I was used to crows so I thought little of their raucous "caw-caws" until one sounded near my head.

Before I could do anything to save myself, a sharp, pointed beak was pecking at my face.

Suddenly I felt myself hoisted into the air by my waistband. I tried to cling to the tree roots, but it was no use. They sank away from me as I

rose feet first. My skirts crackled in the wind
as it rushed past, and I felt myself go up,
now down.

'This is certainly the end of me!' I
thought to myself.

I came to rest at last and I found myself
in a great untidy nest at the top of a pine
tree, staring into the surprised faces of three
half-grown crows. They may not
have been so large and fierce
as their mother, but they
made up for this by their
hoarse cries for food
and their gaping
red throats. I
was jostled

and crowded and poked and shoved until it seemed there would be nothing left of me.

How I ever survived that first night I do not know, but morning came at last. It was strange to see the sun rise behind the topmost branches of a pine, and to feel the nest rocking as the branches swayed in the wind. Little by little I learned to climb higher so that I might peer out over the nest's edge. This terrified me at first, so that I dared not look down from such a vast height. That was why it took me such a long time to discover that I was not far from home, as I had supposed, but within a stone's throw of my own front door.

There was comfort in this at first. Later, it seemed only to make things harder. To see the Preble family moving about below me, to hear the voices of Andy and Phoebe, and yet to be unable to attract their attention was tantalizing. And still the baby crows squawked and shoved and fought. I grew more uncomfortable and lonely as the day wore on.

Night came on. The stars shone very clear and big, like snow crystals sprinkled across the dark sky.

"I cannot bear it any longer," I told myself at last. "Better be splintered than endure this for another night."

I knew that any move must be made at once, before the mother crow returned from a last late expedition. So I began working my way towards the edge of the nest. I must

confess that I have never been
more frightened in my life than
when I peered down into that
vast space below and thought of
hurling myself into it. Just for a
moment my courage failed me.

"Nothing ventured, nothing
gained," I reminded myself.

"Caw, caw, caw!"

I heard the mother
crow coming and knew
there was not a moment to lose.
Fortunately for me, the young crows
heard this too, and began flinging
themselves about the nest so violently that
I could not have stayed in if I had wanted
to. Up went my two feet, out went my

arms, and plop! I dropped over the edge of
the nest!

The darkness seemed like a bottomless
pit into which I was falling.
Stiff pine needles and cones
scratched my face and
sharp twigs tore at me as
I fell down, down, down. By
the time I stopped I thought I
must certainly have reached
the bottom. But I felt pine
needles and branches
about me, and when
I stretched out my
arms there was

no comforting solid earth between them.

Instead of falling clear of the old pine, as I had expected, I had become entangled in one of the outer branches. There I dangled in midair with my head down and my petticoats over it.

I soon discovered that although I could see plainly everything that went on about the Preble house, I might have been a pine cone for all the notice I got. It never occurred to one of the family to stand underneath the pine tree and look for me in such a place.

So I hung there for a number of days and nights, headfirst, drenched by rains and buffeted by every wind that blew by.

'Suppose,' I thought sadly, 'I have to hang

here till my clothes fall into tatters. Suppose
they never find me until Phoebe is grown
up and too old for dolls.'

I know she missed me. I heard her tell
Andy so, and he promised to go once more
with her to look for me.

Curiously enough, it was the crows who
were the means of reuniting us in the end.
They had begun to try their own wings.
Such flapping and cawing they made, too.
Never have I heard anything like it.
Mrs Preble said their goings-on were
driving her distracted, and Andy spent most
of his time aiming at them with pebbles and
a sling shot.

Finally, one morning when Andy stood
right under the old pine with his sling shot

all poised and ready, he caught sight of me.

"Phoebe!" he screamed, "come and see what's growing on the old pine."

Soon the whole family were all gathered in a group under me discussing the best way to bring me back to earth.

Then Captain Preble appeared with a long pole he had cut. This was tall enough to reach me and to my joy I felt myself lifted free of the pine bough.

"I wouldn't wonder but those pesky crows fetched her away," Andy told Phoebe.

But Phoebe was too happy to have me back to bother about that.

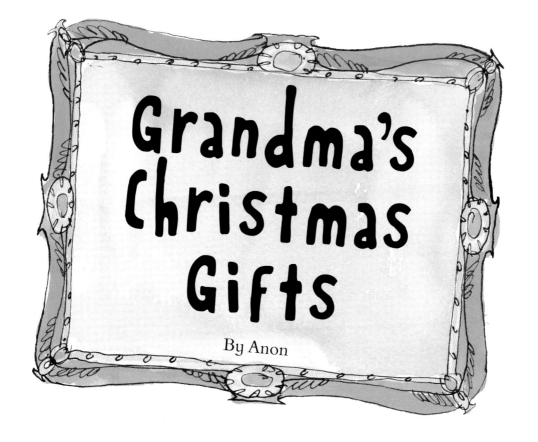

Grandma's Christmas Gifts

By Anon

GRANDMA BURNS sat knitting one bright morning the week before Christmas. The snow lay deep and the hard crust glistened like silver. All at once she heard little sighs and sobs outside her door. When she opened it there sat Peter and Jimmy Rice, two poor little boys, with their faces in their hands and they were crying.

"What can be the matter with two little boys this sunny morning?" asked Grandma.

"We don't have any good times," sighed little Peter.

"We haven't any sleds," sighed Jimmy.

"Why, of course boys can't have a good time without sleds," said Grandma, cheerily. "Let us look about and see if we can't find something." And Grandma's head bobbed behind barrels and boxes in the shed, and all among the cobwebs in the garret, but nothing suitable could be found.

"I do believe this would do for Peter,"
and the dear old lady drew a large, tin pan
off the top shelf in the pantry. A long,
smooth tray was found for Jimmy.

Grandma shook her head with laughter
to see them skim over the hard
crust in their strange sleds.
And the boys shouted and
swung their hands as they
flew past the window.

"I do expect they'll
wear them

through," murmured Grandma, "but boys must slide, that's certain."

And the pan was scoured as bright as a new silver dollar, and the red paint was all gone off the wooden tray, when Peter and Jimmy brought their sleds back.

Grandma knitted faster than ever all that day, and her face was bright with smiles. She was planning something. She went to see the carpenter that night, and he promised to make two small sleds in return for the pair of socks she was knitting.

When the sleds were finished she painted them red and drew a yellow horse upon each one (Grandma called them horses, but no one would have known it). Then the night before Christmas she drew on her

snow boots to keep her from slipping, put
on her hood and cloak, and dragged the
little sleds over to Peter and Jimmy's house.

She hitched them to the door-latch, and
then went home, laughing all the way.

Raggedy Andy to the Rescue

By Johnny Gruelle

*Raggedy Andy, Raggedy Ann and the other toys
live with their owner, a little girl called Marcella.
The penny dolls are two very little dolls.*

ALL DAY SATURDAY the men had worked out upon the eaves of the house, and the dolls facing the window could see them.

The men made quite a lot of noise with

their hammers, for they were putting new gutters around the eaves, and pounding upon metal makes a great deal of noise.

After the men had left their work and gone home, the house was quiet. Raggedy Andy cautiously moved his head out from under the little bed quilt and, seeing that the coast was clear, sat up. This was a signal for all the dolls to sit up.

The nursery window was open, so Raggedy Andy lifted the penny dolls to the windowsill and climbed up beside them. Leaning out, he could look along the new, shiny tin gutter the men had put in place.

"Here's a grand place to have a lovely slide," he said, as he gave one of the penny dolls a scoot down the shiny tin gutter.

"Whee! See her go!" Raggedy Andy cried excitedly.

All the other dolls climbed upon the windowsill beside him.

"Scoot me too!" cried the other penny doll in her squeaky little voice. And so Raggedy Andy took her in his rag hand and gave her a great swing, which sent her scooting down the new, shiny tin gutter, "Kerswish!"

Then Raggedy Andy climbed into the gutter himself and, taking a few steps, spread out his feet and went scooting down the shiny tin.

The other dolls scooted along behind him. When Raggedy Andy came to the place where he expected to find the penny dolls lying, they were nowhere to be seen.

"Perhaps you scooted them farther than you thought," Uncle Clem said.

"Perhaps I did," Raggedy Andy said anxiously. "We will look around the bend."

"Oh dear!" he exclaimed when he had peeped around the corner of the roof. "The gutter ends here and there is nothing but a hole!"

"They must have scooted right into that hole," Henny, the Dutch doll, said.

Raggedy Andy lay flat upon the shiny tin and looked down into the hole.

"Are you down there, penny dolls?" he called loudly.

There was no answer.

"I'm so sorry I scooted them!" Raggedy Andy cried. "Maybe if you hold onto my feet, I can reach down the hole and find them. And then I can pull them up again," he said.

Uncle Clem and Henny each caught hold of one of Raggedy Andy's feet, and let him slide down into the hole.

It was a rather tight fit, but Raggedy Andy wiggled and twisted until all the dolls could see of him were his two feet.

"I can't find them," he said in muffled

tones. "Let me down farther and I think I'll be able to reach them."

Now Henny and Uncle Clem thought that Raggedy Andy meant for them to let go of his feet, and this they did.

Raggedy Andy kept wiggling and twisting until he came to a bend in the pipe and could go no farther.

"I can't find them!" he cried. "They have gone farther down the pipe. Now you can pull me up."

"We can't reach you, Raggedy Andy!" Uncle Clem called down the pipe. "Try to wiggle back up."

Raggedy Andy tried to wiggle backwards up the pipe, but his clothes caught upon a little piece of tin that stuck out from the inside of the pipe, and there he stayed. He could neither go down nor come back up.

"What shall we do?" Uncle Clem cried. "The folks will never find him down there, for we cannot tell them where he is, and they will never guess it."

The dolls were all very sad. They stayed out upon the new, shiny tin gutter until it began raining, and hoped and hoped that Raggedy Andy could get back up to them.

Then they went inside the nursery and sat looking out the window, until it was time for the folks to get up and the house to be astir. Then they went back to the position each had been in when Marcella had left them.

And although they were very quiet, each doll was so sorry to lose Raggedy Andy, and they all felt that he would never be found again.

All day Sunday it rained, and all of Sunday night and Monday morning, when Daddy left for work, it was still raining.

As Daddy walked out of the front gate, he turned to wave goodbye to Mamma and Marcella, and then he saw something.

Daddy came right back into the house and called up the men who had put in the new, shiny tin gutters.

"The drain pipe is plugged up," he told them. "Some of you must have left shavings or something in the eaves, and it has washed down into the pipe, so that the

296

water pours over the gutter in sheets!"

"We will send a man right over to fix it," was the reply.

So at about ten o'clock that morning one of the men came to fix the pipe. He measured with his stick, so that he knew just where the place was, and with a pair of tin shears he cut a section from the pipe. And he found Raggedy Andy!

The man laughed out loud and carried little, water-soaked Raggedy Andy back into the house.

"I guess your little girl must have dropped this rag doll down into the drain pipe," the man said to Mamma.

"I'm so glad you found him," Mamma said to the man. "We have hunted all over the house for him!"

So Mamma put Raggedy Andy behind the radiator, and there he sat all afternoon, steaming and drying out.

And as he sat there he smiled and smiled, even though there was no one to see him.

Raggedy Andy felt very happy within and he liked to smile anyway, because his smile was painted on. But there was another

reason Raggedy Andy smiled, and this was
because he was not alone – inside his belt
were the two little penny dolls.

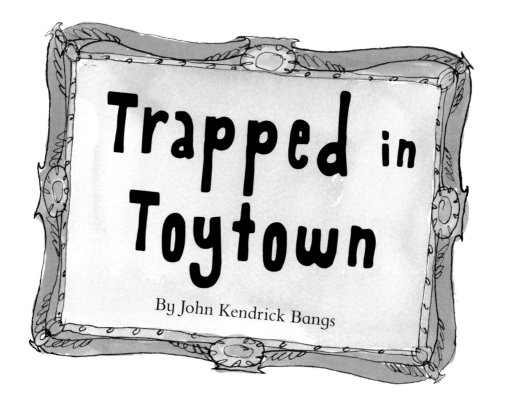

Trapped in Toytown

By John Kendrick Bangs

IT CAME ABOUT in this way Jimmieboy had been a wee bit naughty, and so had to sit in his bedroom. At the end of fifteen minutes, his eye caught sight of a little crack in one corner. As he gazed at it, it seemed to widen, and then what should appear at the bottom of it but a little iron gate!

Trapped in Toytown

"That's the strangest thing I've ever seen!" said Jimmieboy, peering through it.

And then a funny little old man came to the other side of the gate and said, "Won't you come in and see what an interesting country we have?"

"Thanks," said Jimmieboy. "What is this place?" he asked, as he gazed about him and noticed that all the houses were made of cake and candy.

"This," said the little old man, clanging the gate and locking it, "is Toyland, and you are my prisoner."

"Your what?" cried Jimmieboy.

"My prisoner is what I said," retorted the little old man. "I keep a toy shop in Toyland, and I'm going to put you in my shop window and sell you to the first big toy that wants to buy you for a Christmas present for his little toy at home."

"I d–don't understand," stammered Jimmieboy anxiously.

"Well, you will in a minute," said the little old man. "We citizens of Toyland have Christmas just as much as you people do. You sell us and we sell you when we catch you – and, what is more, the boy who is kind to his toys in your country finds his toy master in Toyland kind to him. I am told that you are very good to your toys and keep them very carefully, so you needn't be afraid that you will be given to one of our rough toys. Step right in here."

Jimmieboy didn't dare rebel, so he started to do as he was told. He had caught sight of the toy shop window, and what should he see there but his friends Whitty and Billie and Johnnie.

"Great haul of children, eh?" said the little old man. "They'll sell like hot cakes."

"You've got all my friends except Tommy Hicks," said Jimmieboy.

"I know," said the little old man. "We had Tommy this morning, but a toy rabbit came in and bought him to put in his little toy's stocking. He gave me a dollar for Tommy, but I'll charge ten for you. They'll have to pay a good price for Whitty, too, because there's so much goes with him. He's got a collection of stamps and some marbles in one pocket, and a muffin and a picture book in another."

"How did you capture him?" asked Jimmieboy, who felt better now that he saw that he was not alone in this strange land. "Did he come through that crack that I came by?"

"No, indeed," said the little old man. "He climbed into his mamma's pantry after some jam, and while he was there I just turned the pantry around, and he walked right through the door into the back of my shop. There was a doll in here this afternoon who wanted to buy him for her daughter, but she only had $8, and I'm not going to let Whitty go for less than $12, considering all the things he's brought with him."

Then Jimmieboy entered the shop. Instead of there being toys on the shelves waiting to be bought, there were children lying there, while the toys were walking up and down. The salesmen were all elves. Jimmieboy was too interested in what he saw to feel very anxious, and so he asked the little old man very cheerfully what he should do.

"Step right into the window and sit down," said the little old man. "Smile cheerfully, and once in a while get up and twirl around on your right leg. That will attract the attention of the toys, and maybe

one of them will come in and buy you.
Can you sing?"

"Yes," said Jimmieboy. "Why?"

"I wanted to know so that I could
describe you properly," said the little old
man. "Would you like to be called the
Automatic Musical Jimmieboy?"

"Yes, that would be fine,"
replied Jimmieboy.

"Whenever anybody wants
to see you, you must sing.
That's what I mean by
calling you an
Automatic Musical
Jimmieboy – you are a
Jimmieboy that sings
of its own accord."

306

Trapped in Toytown

So Jimmieboy got into the
window, where, for hours, he was
stared at by rag dolls, toy soldiers,
knitted monkeys, and all sorts of
other toys who lived in this strange
land, and who were walking on the
sugared sidewalk.

One woollen monkey called in to
ask his price, but the monkey found
him too expensive, for, as you may
already know, woollen monkeys
don't usually have as much as $10 in
their pockets.

A little later a wooden
Noah came in and bought
Whitty, and Jimmieboy
began to feel tired and

lonely. Some of the toys in the street made faces at him. A toy lion said he thought he'd go in and take a bite of him, he looked so good, which Jimmieboy didn't like at all.

Finally he was sold to a doll, and the next thing he knew he was put in a box to be sent by post to the doll's cousin. Jimmieboy didn't like this at all, and as the little old man tied the string that fastened him in the box, he kicked hard. Freeing his arms from the paper, Jimmieboy sprang up and began laying about him with his fists. The little old man ran away in terror. The doll changed his mind and said he didn't think he wanted the Automatic Musical Jimmieboy after all, and left.

Jimmieboy grabbed up three of the elves,

who were trying to hide in the fire extinguisher, rushed out of the shop and landed – where do you suppose?

Back in his own room!

How the room got there or what became of the elves he does not know to this day, but it is from him that I got the story. The oddest thing about it, though, is that Whitty has no memory of the adventure at all, which is really very strange, for Whitty has a marvellous memory.

Child's Play

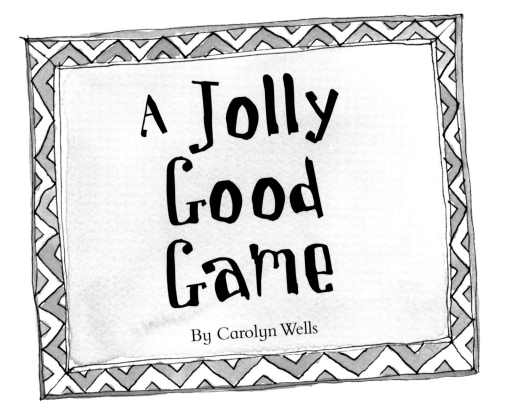

A Jolly Good Game

By Carolyn Wells

"**W**HAT DO YOU SAY, KINGDON?"

"I say shipwreck, on an awfully desert island."

"I say shipwreck, too," said Kitty.

"All right," agreed Marjorie, "shipwreck, then. I'll get the coconuts."

"Me, too," chimed in Rosy Posy. "Me

312

A Jolly Good Game

tumble in the wet water, too!"

The speakers were the four Maynard children, and they were deciding on their morning's occupation. It was a gorgeous day in early September. Shipwreck was always a favourite, because it could develop in so many ways. Once they were shipwrecked, no rescue was possible unless real help appeared. It might be a neighbour's child coming to see them, or one of their own parents, but they must be really rescued by actual outsiders.

The desert island was selected, and they chose a small grassy hill under an old maple tree.

Marjorie disappeared in the direction of the kitchen and, after a time, came back with a small basket, apparently well-filled.

With this she scampered away to the desert island, and soon returned, swinging the empty basket.

Then the four children went to the double wooden swing and got in. Kitty carried her doll, Arabella, and Rosy Posy hugged her big white teddy bear, who was called Boffin. Today, the swing was an ocean steamer.

Soon they were all on board and the ship started. At first all went smoothly. The swing swayed gently and the passengers admired the beautiful scenery.

"I'm not afraid of the sea," said Marjorie, "as much as I am of that fearful wild bear. Will he bite?"

A Jolly Good Game

"No," said Kingdon, looking at Rosy Posy. "That's his trainer who is holding him. He's – he's Buffalo Bill. Speak up, Rosy Posy, you're Buffalo Bill, and that's a bear you're taking home to your show."

"Ess," said Rosamond, "I'se Buffaro Bill, an' 'is is my big, big bear."

But then the ship began to pitch and toss fearfully. Kingdon yelled, "We're on a rock! The ship is settling! Launch the boats!"

The four children screamed and groaned, the swing shook violently then came almost to a standstill.

Kingdon fell out with a bounce and lay on the ground. Marjorie sprang out and, as she reached the ground, struck out like a swimmer in the water.

Kitty daintily stepped out with her doll, remarking, "This is a fine life jacket. I can stand up in the water!"

Baby Rosamond bundled out backwards, dropping Boffin as she did so.

"The bear, the bear!" screamed Kingdon. And swimming a few strokes along the soft, green grass, he grabbed the bear and waved him.

Buffalo Bill frequently forgot she was in the tossing ocean, and walked upright on her own little legs.

A Jolly Good Game

At last by a mighty effort, they
managed to reach the shore of the
island. Exhausted, Marjorie
threw herself on the beach, and
the half-drowned Kingdon also
dragged himself up on dry land.
"We have escaped one
terrible death," he declared, "only
to meet another! We will starve!
This is a desert island exactly in the
middle of the Pacific Ocean."

"Oh! What shall we do?" moaned
Kitty. "My precious Arabella! Already she is
begging for food."

"If there is nothing else," said Marjorie,
"we must kill the bear and eat him."

"No, no!" screamed baby Rosamond.

"No, no eat my Boffin Bear."

"I will explore," said Kingdon. "Come Buffalo Bill. Perhaps we will find coconuts."

"Ess," said Buffalo Bill, "an' we'll take Boffin, so he won't get all killded."

The two went away, and returned in a surprisingly short time with a surprising amount of food.

"These are coconuts," announced Kingdon, as he displayed four oranges. "I had to climb the tallest palm trees to reach them."

"Edds," said Rosy Posy, triumphantly, and in her small skirt were three eggs.

"I, too, will make search!" cried Marjorie. She returned with a paper bag of crackers and another of pears.

A Jolly Good Game

"These are bread fruit," she announced, "and these are wild pears. We're lucky to be shipwrecked on such a fruitful island."

"Lucky, indeed!" agreed Kingdon. "Why, when I discovered those eggs, I knew at once they were gulls' eggs."

"And how fortunate that they're boiled," said Kitty.

The shipwrecked sufferers then spread out their food and sat down to a pleasant meal, for the Maynard children could eat at almost any hour of the day.

"Buffaro Bill so s'eepy," announced Rosy Posy and, with Boffin for a pillow, she calmly dropped off into a morning nap.

But the others suffered various dreadful adventures. They were attacked by wild beasts, which, though entirely imaginary, needed almost as much killing as if they had been real.

As noon drew near, the settlers on the island began to grow hungry again and, strange to say, the imaginary birds they shot and ate were not very filling.

Buffalo Bill woke up and demanded a drink of water. But none could leave the island unless in a rescue ship.

For a long time they waited. They waved a white flag and even shouted for help.

At last, they saw a white-covered wagon slowly moving along the back drive.

"Help! Help!" cried all of the four children in chorus.

It was the butcher's wagon and they

A Jolly Good Game

knew it well, but there was a new driver who didn't know the Maynard children.

"What's the matter?" he cried, jumping from his seat and running across the grass.

"We're shipwrecked!" cried Marjorie. "We can't get home. Oh, save us!"

"Help!" cried Kitty, faintly. "My child is ill and I can no longer survive!" Dramatic Kitty sank in a heap on the ground.

"Save me!" cried Rosy Posy. "Save Buffaro Bill first – me an' Boffin Bear."

The butcher's boy picked her up, and with a few long strides reached his cart.

"It's a game," explained Kingdon. "We're shipwrecked on a desert island, and you're a passing captain of a small sailing vessel. Will you take us aboard?"

"Sure, sir," said the butcher's boy. The
four children clambered into the wagon,
and the butcher drove them in triumph to

the back door. Here they jumped out and,
after thanking their rescuer, they scampered
into the house.

A Jolly Good Game

"Such fun!" said Rosy Posy, as her mother bathed her heated little face. "Us was all shipperecked, an' I was Buffaro Bill, an' Boffin was my big wild bear!"

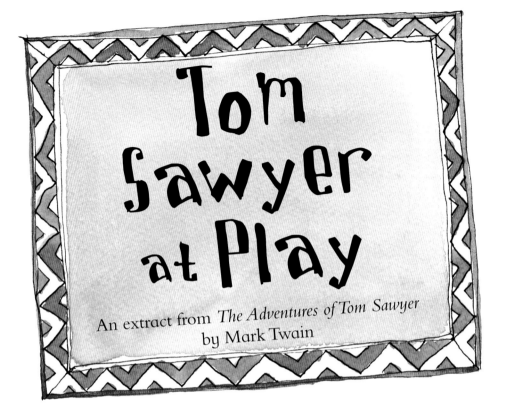

Tom Sawyer at Play

An extract from *The Adventures of Tom Sawyer*
by Mark Twain

*Tom lives in Mississippi in the nineteenth century. He believes
in superstitions and magic, and here he is trying to work a spell to
make his lost marbles come back. Joe Harper is a friend of his and
they like playing at Robin Hood. A shingle is a wooden roof tile.*

HE WENT TO A ROTTEN log near at
hand, and began to dig under one
end of it with his knife. He soon struck
wood that sounded hollow. Tom put his
hand there and uttered this incantation:

"What hasn't come here, come! What's here, stay here!"

Then Tom scraped away the dirt, exposing a pine shingle. He took it up and uncovered a shapely little treasure house, whose bottom and sides were of shingles. In it lay a marble. Tom's astonishment was boundless! He scratched his head and said, "Well, that beats anything!"

Then Tom tossed the marble away and stood thinking. The truth was, a superstition of his had failed here. If you buried a marble with certain necessary incantations, left it alone for a fortnight, and then opened the place with the incantation he had just used, you would find that all the marbles you had ever lost had gathered themselves together in that place.

But now, this thing had actually failed. Tom's faith was shaken. He had many a time heard of this thing succeeding, but never of its failing before. It did not occur to Tom that he had tried it several times before, himself, but could never find the hiding-places afterwards.

Tom puzzled over the matter for some time, and finally decided that some witch had interfered and broken the charm, so he gave up discouraged. But it occurred to him that he might as well have the marble he had just thrown away, and he went and made a patient search for it. But he could not find it.

Now he went back to his treasure house

and carefully placed himself just as he had been standing when he tossed the marble away. Then he took another marble from his pocket and tossed it in the same way, saying, "Brother, go find your brother!"

Tom watched where it stopped, and went there and looked. But the marble must have fallen short or gone too far, so he tried twice more. The last repetition was successful – two marbles lay within a foot of each other.

Just then the blast of a toy tin trumpet came faintly down the green aisles of the forest. Tom flung off his jacket and trousers, turned his scarf into a belt, raked away some brush behind the rotten log to uncover a bow and arrow, a wooden sword and a tin trumpet, and in a moment had seized these things and bounded away, barelegged, with a fluttering shirt.

He presently halted under a great elm, blew an answering blast, and then began to tiptoe and look warily out, this way and that. He said cautiously, to an imaginary company, "Hold, my merry men! Keep hidden until I blow."

Now Joe Harper appeared, dressed and armed like Tom.

"Hold! Who comes here into Sherwood Forest without my pass?" Tom called.

"Guy of Guisborne wants no man's pass. Who art thou that – that—"

"Dares to hold such language," said Tom, prompting him, for they talked by the book from memory.

"Who art thou that dares to hold such language?" Joe said.

"I, indeed! I am Robin Hood, as thy carcass soon shall know," replied Tom.

"Then art thou indeed that famous outlaw?" said Joe. "Right gladly will I dispute with thee the passes of the merry wood. Have at thee!"

They took their swords, dumped their other traps on the ground, struck a fencing attitude, foot to foot, and began a grave, careful combat, two up and two down.

Presently Tom said, "Now, if you've got the hang of it, go at it lively!"

So they went at it lively, panting and perspiring with the work. By and by Tom shouted, "Fall! Fall! Why don't you fall?"

"I won't! Why don't you fall yourself? You're getting the worst of it," Joe replied.

"Why, that ain't anything. I can't fall, that ain't the way it is in the book. The book says, 'Then with one back-handed stroke he slew poor Guy of Guisborne.' You're to turn around and let me hit you in the back."

There was no getting around the authorities, so Joe turned, received the whack and fell.

Tom Sawyer at Play

"Now," said Joe, getting up, "you've got to let me kill you. That's fair."

"Why, I can't do that, it ain't in the book."

"Well, it's blamed mean – that's all."

"Well, Joe, you can be Friar Tuck or Much the miller's son, and hit me with a quarter-staff – or I'll be the Sheriff of Nottingham and you be Robin Hood a little while and kill me."

This was satisfactory, and so these adventures were carried out. Then Tom became Robin Hood again, and was allowed, by the treacherous nun, to bleed his strength away through his neglected wound.

At last, Joe, representing a whole tribe of weeping outlaws, dragged him sadly forth, gave his bow into his feeble hands, and Tom said, "Where this arrow falls, there bury poor Robin Hood under the greenwood tree." Then he shot the arrow and fell back. He would have died, but he fell on a nettle and sprang up too gaily for a corpse!

The boys dressed themselves and went off grieving that there were no outlaws any more. They said they would rather be outlaws for a year in Sherwood Forest than President of the United States forever.

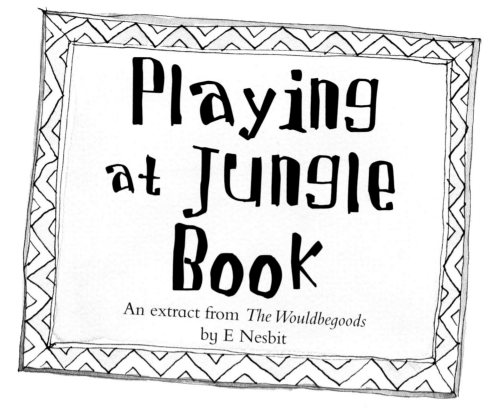

Playing at Jungle Book

An extract from *The Wouldbegoods*
by E Nesbit

*The Bastable children, Oswald, Dora, Dicky, Alice, Noel
and H.O., are staying with their father's friend, who they call
'the uncle'. Two timid children, Daisy and Denny, are staying
with them. A beer stand is a wooden frame to hold a beer barrel.*

NEXT MORNING, when we were having
breakfast, Oswald suddenly said,
"I know, we'll have a jungle in the garden!"
Then he continued, "We'll play Jungle
Book! I shall be Mowgli and the rest of you

333

can be what you like."

We all agreed to make the jungle first and dress up for our parts afterwards. Of course, the shrubbery was to be the jungle, and the lawn under the cedar would be a forest glade. And then we began to collect the things.

We all thought of different things. First we dressed up pillows in the skins of beasts and set them about on the grass to look as natural as we could. Denny helped with the wild beast skins, and said, "Please may I make some paper birds to put in the trees? I know how."

Of course we all said yes, and so timid Denny quickly made quite a lot of large paper birds with red tails. But while he was doing this he suddenly said, or rather screamed, "Oh?"

We looked and it was a creature with great horns and a fur rug – something like a bull and also something like a minotaur – and I don't wonder Denny was frightened. But it was only Alice, and it was first-class.

Oswald undid the back of the glass case in the hall, and got out the stuffed fox with the green and grey duck in its mouth. When the

335

others saw how awfully life-like they looked on the lawn, they all rushed off to fetch the other stuffed things. The uncle really has a tremendous lot of stuffed animals. The duck-bill – what's its name? – looked very well sitting on his tail with the otter snarling at him.

Then Dicky got the hose and put the end over a branch of the cedar tree. We got the step ladder they clean windows with, and let the hose rest on the top of them. Then we got Father's and the uncle's raincoats and covered the step ladder with them, so that the water ran down in a stream, away across the grass. The stuffed otter and duck-bill-thing looked just as if they were in their native haunts!

Playing at Jungle Book

I do hope all of this is not very dull to read about. I know it was jolly good fun for us to do.

We got all the rabbits out of their hutches and put pink paper tails on them. They got away somehow, and before they were caught the next day, they had eaten a good many lettuces and other things.

Denny put paper tails on the guinea pigs. One of the guinea pigs was never seen again, and the same could be said for the tortoise, after we had painted his shell a brilliant red. He crawled away and returned no more.

The lawn under the cedar was transformed into a dream of beauty, what with all of the stuffed animals, the waterfall and the pink paper-tailed rabbits and guinea pigs.

Alice said, "I wish the tigers did not look so flat." For of course with pillows you can only pretend it is a sleeping tiger, not one getting ready to make a spring out at you. It is very difficult to prop up tiger skins in a life-like manner when there are no bones inside them.

"What about the beer stands?" I said. And so we got two out of the cellar, and with string we fastened them to the tigers – they were really fine.

Then H. O. painted his legs and his hands to make himself brown, so that he might be Mowgli. Although Oswald had clearly said earlier that he was going to be

Mowgli himself.

Of course the others weren't going to stand that. So Oswald said, "Very well. Nobody asked you to brown yourself like that. But now you've done it, you've got to go and be a beaver, and live in the dam under the waterfall."

Noel said, "Don't make him. Let him be the bronze statue that the fountain plays out of."

So we let him have the hose and hold it up over his head. It made a lovely fountain.

Then Dicky and Oswald and I did ourselves brown too. The brown did not come off any of us for days.

Oswald was to be Mowgli, and we were just beginning to arrange the different parts.

The rest of the hose that was on the ground was Kaa, the python. While most of us were talking, Dicky and Noel got messing about with the beer stand tigers.

And then a really sad event instantly occurred, which was not really our fault, and we did not mean to.

That Daisy girl had been mooning indoors all the afternoon, and now she suddenly came out, just as Dicky and Noel had got under the tigers and were shoving them along to frighten each other. They did look jolly like real tigers. What happened then was truly horrid.

As soon as Daisy saw the tigers she stopped short, and fell flat on the ground.

Then we were truly frightened. Dora and

Alice lifted her up, and her mouth was a violet colour and her eyes were half shut. She looked horrid.

We did what we could. We rubbed her hands. And we were all doing what we could as hard as we could, when we heard the click of the front gate. There was no mistake about it.

There were feet on the gravel, and there was the uncle's voice, saying in his hearty manner, "This way. This way."

And then, without further warning, the uncle, three other gentlemen and two ladies burst upon the scene.

We had no clothes on to speak of – I mean us boys. We were all wet through. Daisy was in a faint or a fit, or dead, none of us then knew which. And all the stuffed animals were there, staring the uncle in the face. Most of them had got a sprinkling, and the otter and the duck-bill-thing were simply soaked. And some of us were painted dark brown!

"What's all this?" said the uncle.

Oswald spoke up and said it was Jungle Book we were playing, and he didn't know what was up with Daisy. He explained as well as anyone could, but words were now in vain.

When Father came home we got a good talking to, and we said we were sorry – and we really were – especially about Daisy. We promised that in the future we would be good.

It turned out Daisy was not really dead at all. It was only fainting.

I have not even told you half the things we did for the jungle – for instance, about sofa cushions and the uncle's fishing boots!

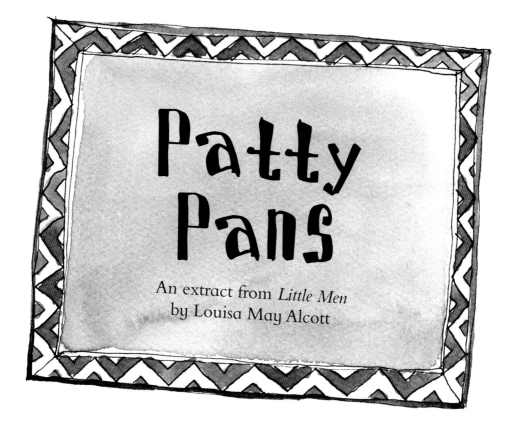

Patty Pans

An extract from *Little Men*
by Louisa May Alcott

*Aunt Jo (also called Mrs Bhaer) runs a school for boys and looks
after her niece, Daisy. She also has a little boy called Teddy,
named after his Uncle Teddy.*

"**W**HAT'S THE MATTER, DAISY?"
asked Aunt Jo.

"I'm tired of playing alone!" Daisy said.

"I'll play with you later, but just now I
must get ready for a trip into town. What

will you do with yourself while I go?"

"I don't know. I'm tired of dolls. I wish you'd make up a new play for me, Aunt Jo," said Daisy.

"I shall have to think of a brand new one, so suppose you go down and see what Asia has got for your lunch," suggested Aunt Jo.

Daisy ran off, and Aunt Jo racked her brain for a new play for her. All of a sudden she seemed to have an idea, for she smiled to herself.

What it was no one found out that day, but Aunt Jo's eyes twinkled when she told Daisy she had thought of a new play, and that she had bought it.

Daisy was very excited and said, "How

can I wait so long? Couldn't I see it today?"

"Oh dear, no! It has got to be arranged. I promised Uncle Teddy that you shouldn't see it until it was all in order."

"If Uncle knows about it then it must be splendid!" cried Daisy.

"Yes, Uncle Teddy went and bought it with me, and we had such fun in the shop choosing the different parts. You must give him your best kiss when he comes, for he is the kindest uncle that ever went and bought a charming little coo – Bless me! I nearly told you what it was!" and Aunt Jo cut herself off in the middle. Then Daisy sat quite still, trying to think what play had a "coo" in it.

Daisy got through the afternoon, went to

bed early, and next morning went to see her
Aunt Jo to have the new play.

"It's all ready, come on," said Aunt Jo,
and she led the way upstairs to the nursery.

"I don't see anything," said Daisy

"Do you hear anything?" asked Aunt Jo.

Daisy did hear an odd crackling, and
then a little sound as of a kettle singing.
These noises came from behind a curtain
drawn before a deep bay window. Daisy
snatched it back quickly, gave one joyful
"Oh!" and then stood gazing at, what do
you think?

A wide seat ran around the three sides of
the window. On one side hung little pots
and pans, on the other side there was a
small dinner and tea set, and in the middle

part a cooking stove, a real stove, big enough to cook for a large family of very hungry dolls. But the best of it was that a real fire burned in it. Just above the stove hung a dustpan and brush, a little market basket was on the low table, and over the back of a little chair hung a white apron.

Daisy stood still after the first glad "Oh!" then the happy little girl hugged her Aunt Jo, saying gratefully, "Oh Aunty, it's a splendid new play! It's the sweetest, dearest kitchen in the world. Can I learn pies, and cake, and macaroni, and everything?"

"All in good time. I thought I'd see if I could find a little stove for you, and teach you to cook. That would be fun, and useful too. I shall tell you what to do and show you how."

"Oh, what shall I do?" asked Daisy, impatient to begin.

"Shut the stove, so that the oven may heat up. Then wash your hands and get out the flour, sugar, salt, butter and cinnamon. See if the pie board is clean, and then peel your apple ready to put in."

Daisy got things together with as little noise and spilling as could be expected from so young a cook.

"Take that little pan full of flour and then rub in as much butter as will go on that plate," Aunt Jo said.

"I know how. Don't I butter the pie plates as well?" asked Daisy, whisking the flour about.

"Quite right! I do believe you have a gift for cooking," said Aunt Jo, approvingly. "Now scatter some flour on the board and roll the pastry out – yes, that's the way."

Daisy rolled and rolled with the delightful little pin and, having got her pastry, covered the plates with it. Next the apple was sliced in, sugar and cinnamon sprinkled over it, and then the top crust was put on.

"I always wanted to cut them round. How nice it is to do it all by myself!" said Daisy, as the little knife went clipping round the doll's pie plate poised on her hand. "Now I put them in!" she exclaimed, and with an air of triumph she shut the pies in the little oven.

"Clear up your things," Aunt Jo said. "Then peel your squash and potatoes. Cut the potatoes up, so they will go into the little pot. Then put on your vegetables, set the table, and get ready to cook the steak."

What a thing it was to see the potatoes bobbing about in the little pot, to peep at the squash getting soft so fast in the tiny steamer, to whisk open the oven door every five minutes to see how the pies got on, and to put two real steaks in a tiny pan, then proudly turn them with a fork.

The potatoes were done first. They were pounded up with a little pestle, had much butter put in, then put in the oven to brown.

So interested had Daisy been, that she forgot her pastry until she opened the oven door to put in the potato. Then a wail arose, for alas! The little pies were burned black!

"Oh, my pies! My darling pies! They are all spoilt!" cried poor Daisy.

"Dear, dear, I forgot to remind you to take them out," said Aunt Jo. "Don't cry, darling, we'll try again after dinner," she added, as a tear dropped from Daisy's eye and sizzled on the hot ruins of a pie.

"Put the meat dish and your own plates down to warm, while you mash the squash with butter, salt, and a little pepper on the top," said Aunt Jo, hoping that the dinner would meet with no further disasters.

The dinner was safely put upon the table, the six dolls were seated three on a side, Teddy took the bottom, and Daisy the top. One doll was in full ball costume, another in her nightgown. Jerry, the boy, wore his red winter suit, while Annabella, the darling, was dressed in nothing but her own skin.

Teddy, as father of the family, smilingly ate everything offered to him, and did not find a single fault. The steak was so tough that the little carving knife would not cut it, the potato did not go round, and the squash was very lumpy, but the master and mistress of the house cleared the table.

"That is the nicest lunch I ever had. Can't I do it every day?" asked Daisy, as she scraped up and ate the leavings.

"You can cook things every day after lessons," said Aunt Jo, who had enjoyed the dinner party very much, even though no one had invited her to it.

"It is the dearest play ever made!" cried Daisy. "I just wish everybody had a sweet cooking stove like mine."

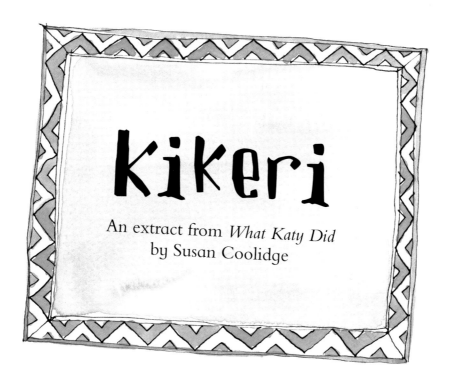

kikeri

An extract from *What Katy Did*
by Susan Coolidge

Katy Carr is part of a large family. Her brothers are Phil and Dorry, and her sisters are Clover, Elsie and John (short for Joanna). The children are looked after by their Aunt Izzie, who is kind but strict. The smaller children sleep together in the nursery.

THIS PARTICULAR MONDAY was rainy, so there couldn't be any outdoor play. Philly was not well and had been taking medicine. It was a great favourite with Aunt Izzie, who kept a bottle of it always on

357

hand. The bottle was large and black, and the children shuddered at the sight of it.

After Philly had stopped roaring and spluttering, and play had begun again, the dolls, as was only natural, were taken ill also. And so was Pikery, John's little yellow chair, which she always pretended was a doll too. John kept an old apron tied on Pikery's back, and generally took him to bed with her – not into bed, but close by, tied to the bedpost.

Now, as she told the others, Pikery was very sick indeed. He must have some medicine, just like Philly.

"Give him some water," suggested Dorry.

"No," said John, "it must be black and out of a bottle, or it won't do any good."

kikeri

After thinking a moment, she trotted quietly across the passage into Aunt Izzie's room. The children were enchanted when she marched back, the bottle in one hand, the cork in the other, and proceeded to pour a dose onto Pikery's wooden seat, which John called his lap.

"There! There! My poor boy," she said, patting his shoulder – I mean his arm! "Swallow it down – it'll do you good."

Just then Aunt Izzie came in. To her dismay she saw a trickle of something dark and sticky running down onto the carpet.

It was Pikery's medicine, which he had refused to swallow.

"What is that?" she asked sharply.

"My baby is sick," faltered John, displaying the guilty bottle.

She scolded them and declared they were troublesome children, who couldn't be trusted one moment out of sight, and that she was more than half sorry she had promised to go out that evening. "How do I know that before I come home you won't have set the house on fire?" she said.

"Oh, no we won't!" whined the children. But ten minutes afterwards they had forgotten all about it.

Supper passed off successfully, Aunt Izzie went out, and all might have gone well, had

Kikeri

it not been that after their lessons, the children fell to talking about Kikeri.

Kikeri was a game that had been very popular with them a year before. They had invented it themselves. It was a sort of mixture of Blindman's Buff and Tag – only instead of anyone's eyes being blindfolded, they all played in the dark.

One of the children would stay out in the hall, which was dimly lit from the stairs, while the others hid themselves in the nursery. When they were all hidden, they would call out "Kikeri" as a signal for the one in the hall to come in and find them.

Of course, coming from the light he could see nothing, while the others could see only dimly. It was very exciting to stand crouching up in a corner, watching the dark figure stumbling about and feeling to the right and left.

Every now and then somebody, just escaping his clutches, would slip past into the hall, which was Freedom Castle, with a joyful shout of "Kikeri, Kikeri, Kikeri, Ki!" Whoever was caught had to take the place of the catcher. Talking of it now put it into their heads to want to try it again.

So they all went upstairs. Dorry and John, though half undressed, were allowed to join the game. Philly was fast asleep in another room.

It was certainly splendid fun. Once Clover climbed up onto the mantelpiece and sat there, and when Katy, who was the catcher, groped about a little more wildly than usual, she caught hold of Clover's foot, and couldn't imagine where it came from. Dorry got a hard knock and cried, and another time Katy's dress caught on the bureau handle and was frightfully torn. But these were too much affairs of every day to interfere in the least with the pleasures of playing Kikeri.

The fun seemed to grow greater the longer they played. In the excitement, time went on much faster than any of them dreamed. Suddenly, in the midst of the noise, there came a sound – the sharp, distinct slam of the door at the side entrance. Aunt Izzie had returned.

The dismay and confusion of that

moment! Aunt Izzie was on her way up stairs, and there was such a panic in the nursery! Katie scuttled off to her own room, where she went to bed with all possible speed. But the others found it much harder to go to bed – there were so many of them, all getting into each other's way, and with no lamp to see by.

Aunt Izzie, coming in with a candle in her hand, gave Clover a sharp scolding. Leaving her to wash her face, Aunt Izzie went to the bed where John and Dorry lay, fast asleep, and snoring as loudly as they knew how. Something strange in the appearance of the bed made her look more closely – she lifted the clothes, and there, sure enough, they were half dressed and

kikeri

with their school shoes on.

Much against their will, John and Dorry were forced to wake up, be scolded and made ready for bed, Aunt Izzie standing over them all the while, like a dragon.

Katy did not even pretend to be asleep when Aunt Izzie went to her room. Her conscience had woken up, and she was lying in bed, very miserable at the failure of setting an example to the younger ones.

The next day, Papa called them together and made them understand that Kikeri was not to be played any more. It was so seldom that Papa forbade any games, however boisterous, that this order really made an impression on the children. They never have played Kikeri again, from that day to this.

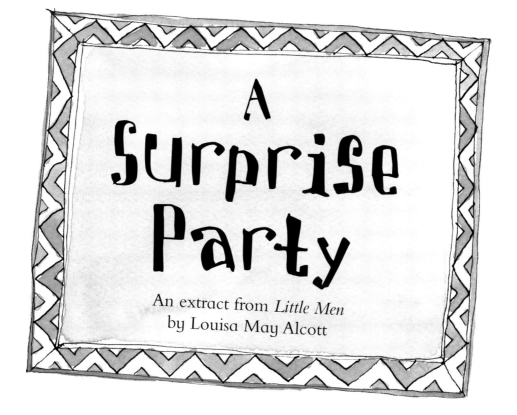

A Surprise Party

An extract from *Little Men*
by Louisa May Alcott

*Aunt Jo (also called Mrs Bhaer) runs a school for boys,
including her nephew Demi, and two boys called Tommy and Nat.
It also has a few girls – her niece, Demi's twin, Daisy, a tomboy
called Nan and Daisy's cousin, Bess.*

"**PLEASE, AUNT JO,** would you and the
girls come out to a surprise party we
have made for you? Do, it's a very nice one."

"Thank you, we will come with pleasure.
Only, I must take Teddy with me," replied

Aunt Jo, with a smile.

"We'd like to have him. The little wagon is all ready for the girls. You won't mind walking just up to Pennyroyal Hill, will you Aunt Jo?"

"Thank you kindly, sir," and Aunt Jo made him a grand curtsey.

Everyone bustled about, and in five minutes the three little girls and Teddy were packed into the clothes basket, as they called the wicker wagon, which Toby drew.

Demi walked at the head of the procession, and Aunt Jo brought up the rear. The three girls had little flutters of excitement all the way there, and Teddy was so charmed with the drive that he kept dropping his little hat overboard.

A Surprise Party

When they came to the hill "nothing was to be seen but the grass blowing in the wind," as the fairy books say, and they all looked disappointed. But Demi said, "Now, you all get out and stand still, and the surprise party will come to you."

A short pause of intense suspense, and then Nat, Demi and Tommy marched forth from behind a rock, each bearing a new kite, which they presented to the three girls. Shrieks of delight arose, but were silenced by the boys, who said, "That isn't all the surprise." And, running behind the rock, they emerged again bearing a fourth kite of superb size, on which was printed, in bright yellow letters, "For Mother Bhaer".

"We thought you'd like one, too," cried

all three, shaking with laughter.

Aunt Jo clapped her hands and joined in the laugh.

"These are magnificent kites. We were wishing we had some the other day, when you were flying yours, weren't we, girls?" Aunt Jo said.

"That's why we made them for you," cried Tommy.

A Surprise Party

"Let us fly them," said energetic Nan.

"I don't know how," began Daisy.

"We'll show you, we want to!" cried all the boys in a burst of devotion, as Demi took Daisy's, Tommy took Nan's, and Nat, with difficulty, persuaded Bess to let go of her little blue one.

"Aunty, if you will wait a minute, we'll pitch yours for you," said Demi.

"Bless your buttons, dear. I know all about it. And here is a boy who will toss it up for me," added Aunt Jo, as the professor peeped over the rock with a face full of fun.

He came out at once, tossed up the big kite, and Aunt Jo ran off with it in fine style, while the children stood and enjoyed the spectacle. One by one all the kites went up and floated far overhead like birds, balancing themselves on the fresh breeze that blew steadily over the hill.

Such a merry time they had! Running and shouting, sending up the kites or pulling them down, feeling them tug at the string like live creatures trying to escape.

Nan was quite wild with the fun. Daisy thought the new play nearly as interesting as dolls. Little Bess was so fond of her "boo tite" that she would only let it go on very short flights, preferring to hold it in her lap. Mrs Jo enjoyed hers immensely. The kite acted as if it knew who owned it, for it came tumbling down head first when least expected, caught on trees, nearly pitched into the river, and finally darted away to

such a height that it looked a mere speck among the clouds.

Eventually everyone got tired, and fastening the kite strings to trees and fences, all sat down to rest.

"Did you ever have such a good time as this before?" asked Nat.

"Not since I last flew a kite, years ago, when I was a girl," answered Aunt Jo.

"I'd like to have known you when you were a girl, you must have been so jolly," said Nat.

"I was a naughty girl, I am sorry to say."

"Tell us about the last time you flew a kite," said Nat, for Aunt Jo had laughed as she spoke of it.

"Oh, it was only rather funny. I was a

A Surprise Party

girl of fifteen, and was ashamed to be seen at such a play. So Uncle Teddy and I privately made our kites, and stole away to fly them. We had a capital time, and were resting as we are now, when suddenly we heard voices, and saw a party of young ladies and gentlemen coming back from a picnic. Teddy did not mind, although he was rather a large boy to be playing with a kite. But I was in a great flurry, for I knew I should be sadly laughed at and never hear the last of it.

"What shall I do?" I whispered to Teddy, as the voices drew nearer and nearer.

"I'll show you," he said, and whipping out his knife he cut the strings. Away flew the kites, and when the people came up we were picking flowers as properly as you please. They never suspected us, and we had a grand laugh over our narrow escape."

"Were the kites lost?" asked Daisy.

"Quite lost, but I did not care," said Aunt Jo, beginning to pull in the big kite, for it was getting late.

"Must we go now?"

"I must, or you won't have any supper!" Aunt Jo replied.

"Hasn't our party been a nice one?" asked Tommy.

"Splendid!" answered everyone.

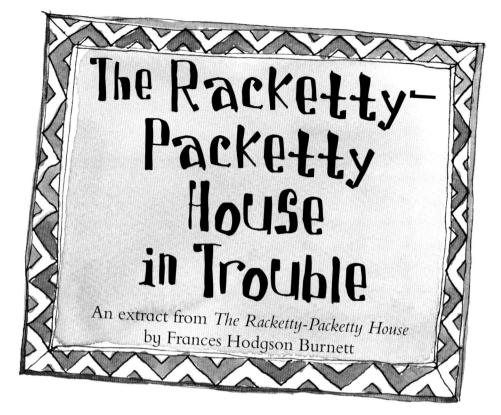

The Racketty-Packetty House in Trouble

An extract from *The Racketty-Packetty House*
by Frances Hodgson Burnett

*The dolls who live in the Racketty-Packetty House are always
scared of being thrown away. But the good fairy who tells this story
looks after them very well. One day one of the dolls, Ridiklis, brings
news for the other dolls that their owner, Cynthia, has gone away.*

"**THE DUCHESS TOLD ME,**" she said,
slowly, because it was bad news. "That
Cynthia went away because her Mamma
sent for her to say that a little princess is
coming to see her tomorrow. Cynthia's

Mamma used to be maid of honour to the Queen and that's why the Princess is coming. The Duchess said—" and here Ridiklis spoke slowly, "that the nurse must tidy the nursery, and have that Racketty-Packetty dolls' house burned in the morning. That's what the Duchess said—"

Meg, Peg, Gustibus and Kilmanskeg clutched at their hearts and gasped.

You can imagine what a sad night it was. They went all over the house, looking at every hole in the carpet, every broken window and chair leg and table, and every ragged blanket – tears ran down their faces.

Now here is where I come in again – Queen Crosspatch – who is telling you this story. I always come in just at the nick of

time when people like the Racketty-
Packetty dolls are in trouble.

An army of my working fairies began to
swarm in at the nursery window. The nurse
was working hard to tidy things, and she
had not sense enough to see fairies at all. As
soon as she made one corner tidy, they
ran after her and made it
untidy. The nurse was so
flurried she forgot all
about Racketty-
Packetty House.
And there it was
when the little
Princess came.

The Princess
was a nice child,

and was polite to Cynthia when she showed her all her dolls, and new dolls' house, Tidy Castle. She looked at the rooms and the furniture and said polite things. But the Princess had so many grand dolls' houses that Tidy Castle did not surprise her at all. It was just as Cynthia was finding this out that I gave the order to my working fairies.

"Push the armchair away very slowly, so that no one will know it is being moved."

So they moved it away – very, very slowly. The next minute the little Princess gave a delightful start.

"Oh! What is that!" she cried out, hurrying towards the house.

Cynthia blushed. The Racketty-Packetty dolls tumbled into a heap by their window.

"It is only a shabby old dolls' house, your Highness," Cynthia stammered. "It belonged to my Grandmamma. I thought you had had it burned, Nurse!"

"Burned!" the Princess cried out. "Why if it was mine, I wouldn't have it burned for worlds! Push the chair away and let me look at it." When the armchair was pushed aside, she scrambled down onto her knees.

"Oh! " she said. "How funny and dear! What a darling old dolls' house. It is shabby and needs mending, but it is almost exactly like one my Grandmamma had – she only let me look at it as a treat."

Cynthia gasped, for the little Princess' Grandmamma had been the Queen.

The Princess picked up Meg and Peg

and Kilmanskeg and Gustibus and Peter Piper as if they had been a Queen's dolls.

"The darling dears," she said. "Look at their nice faces and funny clothes. Just like Grandmamma's dolls' clothes. How I should like to dress them as they used to be dressed, and have the house made as it used to be when it was new."

"That old Racketty-Packetty House," said Cynthia, quietly.

"If it were mine I should make it just like Grandmamma's, and I should love it more than any dolls' house

I have. I never – never – saw anything as nice and laughing and good natured as these dolls' faces. They look as if they have been having fun since they were born. If you were to burn them and their home I – I could never forgive you!"

"I never – never – will – your Highness," stammered Cynthia.

As the Princess liked Racketty-Packetty House so much, Cynthia gave it to her for a present. The Princess was so happy, she made a speech to the Racketty-Packetty family, whom she had set all in a row.

"You will live with me," she said. "And you shall all be dressed beautifully. Your house shall be mended and made as lovely as ever. I will like you better than all my other dolls' houses." Then she was gone.

So Racketty-Packetty House was carried to a nursery in a palace. Meg and Peg and Kilmanskeg and Ridiklis and Gustibus and Peter Piper were made so gorgeous that if they had not been so nice they would have grown proud. But they didn't.

The dolls in the other dolls' houses used to curtsy when a Racketty-Packetty doll passed them. This made Peter Piper want to stand on his head and laugh!

And what do you think of that for a story? Doesn't it prove what a valuable friend a fairy is – particularly a Queen one?